ENTER STAGE WRITE

Stories to Enjoy While We Wait in the Wings

An original collection of short stories
to benefit community theater
in Wilmington, North Carolina

Edited by
Hannibal Hills
&
Kenneth Vest

CONTENTS

This collection published by
Storytellers for Stages
Wilmington, North Carolina
Copyright © 2020
http://storytellersforstages.org
All rights reserved.
ISBN: 9798647423603

"Ace" by Philip Gerard first appeared in
Things We Do When No One Is Watching
BkMk Press, University of Missouri
Kansas City, 2017

FOREWORD

In early 2020, as part of the global isolation to help stop the spread of COVID-19, curtains came down on stages everywhere, with no sense of when they would rise again. Theatre casts, crews, and staff, and productions sometimes years in the planning, were furloughed, leaving many people without income. This brutal necessity left the theatre community wondering and worrying about when, and in many cases if, the footlights might shine again.

In Wilmington, we watched as every stage tearfully posted cancellation notices, and performers took to social media to try their best to keep our spirits up - free of charge - with performances and readings from their own homes. Even as they faced their own personal uncertainty, they showed up, if only virtually, for their audiences. Though the stages were closed, the heart of the theatre community was alive.

Enter Stage Write is one of several projects conjured up locally to help support our fellow artists. Every story included here is an original, very generously donated by the author (most of whom are Wilmington residents). For the audio version, local theatre performers have kindly lent their talents to give voice to the tales.

When the idea to split all proceeds between two local theatre companies - Big Dawg Productions and Panache Productions - was floated among the early supporters of Enter Stage Write, it was warmly received and enthusiastically approved. This, much like the generosity illustrated by the authors and performers involved in this project, is so very Wilmington.

Your purchase of this book will help ensure that the curtain will rise again for new shows, and for those cut short by the pandemic. In the time following the long pause, the artists and leadership of both Big Dawg and Panache will be ready to entertain you, to bring the laughter and applause back to our stages and to our lives. Thank you for your purchase, and for your supporting role in helping to keep theatre alive.

And of course, thank you to all the authors and performers who contributed their valuable time and talent to this book (both the text and audio editions). We are all very fortunate that your generosity is as vast as your passion for the arts.

Hannibal Hills, May 2020

ABOUT BIG DAWG PRODUCTIONS AND PANACHE THEATRICAL PRODUCTIONS

Founded in 1995, Big Dawg Productions, has been committed to producing entertaining, thought-provoking, and socially responsible theater, with an emphasis on education and the promotion of the performing arts. Big Dawg's mission goes beyond their strong record of providing leading-edge and critically acclaimed live theater. They are also heavily committed to education and outreach, and in ensuring that live theater is successfully woven into the very fabric of our society. Since 2009, they have managed the Cape Fear Playhouse on Castle Street, in the heart of Wilmington.

Founded in 2015, Panache Theatrical Productions have made it their mission to present quality theatrical productions that are unique and thought provoking. In doing so, they have produced some the most acclaimed, applauded, and award-winning shows from the past few years, and helped introduce the Wilmington community to many new shows and performers, as well as reviving a few fun theatrical traditions.

Both Big Dawg and Panache are 501(c)3 non-profit organizations.

If you'd like to learn more about these two wonderful theatre companies, please visit them online at:

bigdawgproductions.org
panachetheatre.com.

VERY, VERY

MELISSA RANDALL

It's my third time in Paris.

I don't really have a plan, which seems to be the recurring theme of my life right now. I'm just drifting, collecting experiences to curate into stories for this aptly named blog.

When I arrive in the city, it's nearly 6 p.m. local time.

Immediately enveloped by a wave of heat, I decide to treat myself to a cab drive. The driver cranks the air, providing some relief to the white floral dress I bought in Portugal.

It clings to my skin like wet tissue paper.

My Airbnb is in the St. Germain neighborhood, about a five-minute walk to Notre Dame. After dropping off my backpack, I wander.

I snap a few photos of the cathedral, but I don't go in. I've visited twice before on my previous trips to Paris, and don't really feel like going in again. Instead, I linger outside, trying to think about what to do next.

I contemplate walking away from the river, perhaps trying a different route through a new, undiscovered neighborhood. Uncertain, I find myself heading towards the river anyway.

There's just something about the dusky sunlight, and how it's hitting the water.

I start to feel wistful and day-dreamy, and before I can stop it, my mind wanders.

To him.

At the beginning of my trip, I ended a fling back home. While it was never that serious, I found myself extremely fixated on the object of my desire, a friend turned romantic interest with a great laugh and sparkling brown eyes.

However, after attending the wedding of my best friend in the English countryside, and seeing her exchange vows with her husband, I felt a deep sense of loss. What I had always known about this particular relationship surfaced, and despite a desire to continue, I found myself messaging him right after the ceremony. Due to the circumstances, it was a conversation I was unfortunately forced to have over Facebook Messenger.

As I'm walking along the Seine, my unresolved feelings for him surface. I push them away, refusing to feel sad. Because whenever I've visited Paris, it seems I'm always bringing some kind of baggage with me. Some kind of romantic dilemma. The loneliness is especially palpable for me here. Paris, much like love, has always been slow to reveal itself to me.

But putting mild frustration with both aside, I still pursue. It's encouraging to finally be in Paris alone, I decide. The opportunity to see things from my and only my perspective is promising. Not that I have any expectations for my one night here. Tomorrow, I leave for the constant summer daylight of Reykjavik, a place that has always been very quick to show me its quirks and charms. I'm looking forward to that comfort, that feeling of safety and belonging. Paris is standoffish, I decide, taking one last photo of the Seine. I can't recall if I've taken the same photo before.

I decide to try to draw some kind of reward from the universe for my difficult, yet logical romantic choice. So I log back into Tinder when I return to the studio. I've done this frequently when I travel. I'm not promiscuous by any means (many of these dates are very platonic), I just seem to enjoy dates more when there aren't any strings attached. I just hadn't planned on doing it in Paris. So I write a quick bio – in Paris for one night – let's grab a drink, and start swiping through the candidates. Some are fellow travelers and tourists; some, by appearance, are stereotypical Frenchmen.

Instantly, messages. One dark-haired, thin-faced native Parisian asks me where I am. More specifically, which subway stop. Then he asks "what I want," before a series of question marks and "requests" for my address before I even have a chance to reply. I unmatch him.

The second suitor is more subtle. He asks about my trip, how long my stay is. He's attractive, thick, black, curly hair with wide brown eyes. Skin the color of tea. Before I can dig into my interest any further, he invites me to come over to his flat and smoke weed. I tell him I don't smoke. He replies with his metro stop and home address and tells me to come. I unmatch him.

The third and last potential match is a local architect, with the most innocent intentions of them all. After talking for a bit about my visit, his life here, he says he can't meet up this evening because of an early morning meeting. He requests a date the next night, which I have to refuse because of my flight.

"Oh," he replies.

A beat. Instead of the standard "Let me know the next time you're in [fill city in here]!" message most men send, the ones I meet when on trips, his response is different.

"We'll probably never meet," he says.

"Probably not," I reply.

After a few more aggressive messages, I sigh. I close the app and redo my black eyeliner. I decide to head to this local jazz bar, recommended by a relocated Parisian friend. It's called Le Caveau de la Huchette. He described it as cozy, local. I pull it up on Google Maps and see it's within walking distance of the studio. I remember passing by it a few times that day, actually.

The red neon sign, beams amongst a sea of flashing colorful invitations for pizza, sushi, and crepes. They charge me 10 euro to go in. The bar is pretty empty, with an odd mixture of people. The only jazz I hear is through a crackling speaker. Disappointed, I order a glass of Bordeaux.

The bartender, perhaps sensing this, asks if I'd like an entire bottle. I laugh, and sassily respond, "No, just a glass today."

He pulls out a margarita-sized glass.

"This glass?" he slyly asks, with his somewhat weak English.

"No!" I exclaim, giggling.

As soon as I take a sip, I see a dark staircase near the entrance that I'd somehow missed before. With glass in hand, I gingerly make my way down the shadowy, twisting steps. The reveal is a secluded, cavern-like room with a stage. Before long, a band comes on stage. The energy transforms. Sparks. Parisian looking, elegant women glide across the floor. Thin, lanky bow-tied men twirl them around like little ballerinas in jewelry boxes. I just watch.

I feel him before I see him. A tall, obvious fellow tourist wearing sandals and a man purse (not hating, just observing) is inching closer to me. I can almost hear him breathing when he abruptly leans over, beyond the shoulder I'm using to strategically turn my back to him.

"Do you want to dance?" he says clumsily, with a level of assertiveness I'm not comfortable with.

I feel guilty, but the scowl that crosses his face when I refuse subsides validates it. So after the song ends, I move across the room to a secluded bench. I try to see myself outside of myself, a petite, elfish looking girl with choppy, bleached hair. Brown, worn boots. An almost too-short, dancer-inspired dusty pink dress, borrowed from my friend Katie. A tattered black and white striped tank top lazily draped over it.

I'm watching the band, the puffed-up cheeks of the trumpet player. The smooth, intricate movements of the drummer. The floating skirt of the most graceful Parisian woman as she moves across the dance floor, a skirt similar to my dress when, suddenly –

"Oh, so you don't dance?" I hear someone say.

I look beside me, and there's the shortest man I've ever seen in real life. He looks expectant, and if I'm guessing correctly, about 80 years old. His eyes are blue, and almost the same shade as mine. Completely bald. I stand up and realize that he's even shorter than me, and I'm just 5'2.

"I'm not a very good dancer," I apologize.

He scoffs, in the way that only the French seem to be able to.

"Come, come."

I wish I had a video of this encounter, though I don't think I'll ever forget it. What I imagine, perhaps naively, is something similar to Audrey Hepburn dancing in Funny Face. My dress, made for an occasion like this, swirls and twirls up as he spins me. I'm still a clumsy dancer, missing some of his cues, but Jean-Claude (of course that was his name) didn't seem to mind.

A row of handsome men, who are simply sitting and watching the encounter, seem to perk up. One moves next to the bench I was just sitting at, perhaps waiting for me to return to it. But Jean-Claude refuses to give up his clumsy dance partner. At closing time, my cheeks are flushed. Jean-Claude, I learn, through some difficult conversation, was born (or perhaps, owns a home) in Croatia.

He's been to Yellowstone National Park and wants to go to New Orleans. (Or, perhaps, has been there.) He hates new jazz. He curses the movie La La Land, which I had just watched on the plane. I try to tell him that; he just curses it more.

After making sure I get home safely, just a few blocks' walk that I'd probably be fine without his company, I'm not sure what to say as a farewell. I contemplate asking him if he's on Facebook, then realize how ridiculous it would be to ask an old French man if he's on Facebook.

He obviously understands this.

Instead of saying, "We'll probably never meet again," he says,

"You are very, very, very."

He never specifies very what.

I'll never know why he chose to spend his time entertaining a girl nearly 40-50 years his junior. I'll never know what was in it for him. As a goodbye, I just laugh and shrug about it, promising to return to the jazz club again someday. I turn to unlock my front door, and when I glance over my shoulder, he's nowhere to be seen. Gone as quickly as he was to appear.

I realize that although love is still slow to show itself, tonight, it seems Paris has finally trusted me enough to.

∿

MELISSA RANDALL is *a writer based part-time in Wilmington, North Carolina, and part-time in Brooklyn, New York. Currently, she works for the New York Film Academy as a copywriter and is the editor of her own blogs,* Driftyland *and* Driftygal. *She eats way more pasta than you could ever imagine.*

STARS OF STAGE AND SCREEN

JOEL PERRY

I used to work in radio in Los Angeles. One day my boss, Mr. Cutler, asked me, apropos of nothing, "Why there were so many homosexuals in the theater, Joel?" I didn't know where to begin. To me it was like asking why there was air. There are so many gay men in the theater because there are so many gay men in the theater. I mean, think about it. If you're a homo, ya wanna meet other homos, right? Where are they? In the theater!

Growing up, the theater was the one place I could pretend to be something else and literally get applause for it. Most gays have pretended to be something else for so long, it should surprise no one that we're already pretty damn good at it. So there we are, all over the stage and screen. And each other. But it goes beyond that. At least, to me it did.

For me, theater was where magic was not only allowed but demanded, every day. When I woke up at home, I was fat and shy and painfully ordinary, in some vague way a disappointment. But when I walked onto the stage that evening, I was sure, I was right, I was needed, I was special, and I got applause. I wanted to sleep under the ghost light. I wanted my mail delivered backstage. I wanted my life to be lived there forever. I've more or less managed to do just that.

During my teenage years in Wilmington, NC, I was involved in a summer stock company at the college that, each June through August, was like falling into heaven. It was seven weeks of a new show every week. That meant that in the midst of the season we were blocking one show in the morning to get the basic movements down, having lunch, rehearsing a second show in the afternoon, breaking for dinner, and then performing a third show that night. I was in high school, so I wasn't getting paid, but I was working with people who were making $75 a week—professionals!

Every week my summer stock greasepaint family changed roles with the shows we were doing. I wished my birth family could have done that just once. Even if they had turned into The Little Foxes, at least I would have understood what they were about. As it was, my poor parents were struggling to understand me.

I thought it was perfectly normal to be in the shower belting out the most over-the-top song a 14-year old could sing from Man of La Mancha, "Aldonza the Whore." My mom would tap on the bathroom door, "Dear, could you choose some...other song?" Not a problem. Fiddler on the Roof was coming up. I launched into "Tevye's Dream." The Frumah Sarah part, naturally. "Pearls! P-e-a-r-l-s!"

In that production of Fiddler I was, sadly, not Frumah Sarah, but Reb Nochum, the beggar, who has only one lousy line in the opening number and is scenery for the rest of the show. He's the village blind man, but he somehow manages to keep up with the boisterous dancing crowd in "To Life."

During the wedding scene that ends act I, the Cossacks had to smash tables and knock over chairs. Our Cossacks were way too nelly to pull it off, so they were recast as wedding guests and a stagehand the size of Poland was given the part of destroying the wedding. It looked like the Russians had gone out and hired Mongo from Blazing Saddles. Tevye could have saved all of Anat-evka if he'd just come up with that Candy-Gram gimmick.

In Cabaret, I was also scenery. I was cast as a sailor, engagement party guest, and Nazi among other things. It was as Kit Kat Club patrons, thought, that we chorus members made our mark. The director wanted us to smoke real cigars to create the authentic smoky, smelly club atmosphere. None of us had ever smoked a cigar before, and we didn't get them till opening night. Three of us threw up during "Don't Tell Mama."

When I was 16, I was inexplicably cast in Brigadoon as the father of the female lead. I was thrilled to be given the part and I diligently practiced my Scottish brogue until it was truly heinous. Saying lines like "Auch, aye, laddie," it's hard not to sound like a pirate.

It was the last show of the summer stock season, and everyone was utterly exhausted, so this production got very short shrift. We weren't even taught the big climactic number until the day before opening. It was called "Run and Get Him," where all of Brigadoon would vanish forever if we didn't run and get young Harry Beaton and drag his tartaned tuchis back to town. We were blocked to be running like hell all over the huge, perilously high rocks on the set while belting out the song with appropriate drama and alarm. Due to the concentration it took not to kill ourselves on the jagged 20-foot tall rocks combined with the lateness of learning the lyrics, we ended up shout-singing in dire, manly tones, "Run and get him! Run and get him! Run or blumf flumph la de da da hermfin lermun berman! Run and get him!" We may have been inarticulate, but we were most urgent about it.

Later, at the ripe age of 19, I was cast as a muleteer in my second production of Man of La Mancha in a summer stock company in Burnsville, NC. The stage was severely raked, which means on a slant so steep just walking downstage in boots was a feat. The day we blocked the fight scene was a festival of first aid. Nevertheless, we were actors, and by damn, we would pull it off. The director, imported from New York, gave all the other muleteers their instructions for the scene, involving punches, falls, kicks, and various pratfalls. Recalling years of choosing sides for games in P.E., I was the very last to be put into the scene. I could practically hear the director thinking, "What can I do with the sweaty fat kid?" I'm sure he expected me to be excused from the scene because he told me that for this bit I was to get hit in the groin by Don Quixote, then kicked in the butt by Sancho that would send me into a double somersault into a well where I would fall below stage onto an inadequate mattress and quickly roll away so Aldonza could hurl a small wooden barrel after me, all of this happening on a 20-degree tilt. "Can ya do that, kid?" I had no idea, but I loved being in the theater so much that if he had asked me to set myself on fire and fly, I'd by damn give it my best. And you know what? I did it on the first try! The director was so impressed, he thereafter called me "Bobo," which I later learned had been his nickname years earlier when he was a muleteer in the original Broadway production.

During these shows I did character parts and crowds, helped change costumes, ran props, pushed sets, and flew scenery, sometimes all in the same production. Every now and then there were a couple of shows in which I had acting roles large enough to preclude me from doing anything else. Those occasions were the ultimate gifts of affirmation, like being welcomed into Valhalla, only with rented costumes. And always there were terrific parties after the shows.

At these parties I literally sat at the feet of the professional actors while they told wondrous stories of performing shows in real cities like New York, Boston, and Raleigh. These were outrageous, fun, flamboyant people who were thrilling to be around, completely different from the homunculi I lived among. These people's behavior was exotic, strange, mercurial, and exciting, their very existence a romance. If you haven't figured it out yet, they were screaming, alcoholic, maladjusted theater queens. It was gloriously dysfunctional. And every Wednesday, Thursday, Friday, and Saturday night plus Sunday matinee we made magic together out of sweat, paint, canvas, limelight, and love.

How could I choose any other life over this? What other pursuit could be as noble? Where else could I feel half so alive?

So I made a career in the entertainment industry, albeit in a niche most people don't even know exists. I wrote, directed, and produced syndicated radio comedy for DJs across the U.S. and Canada. There's a good chance you've heard my stuff and not known it. I'm proud to say I made people laugh, because I know the oppressive dullness of the ordinary. I still do it because I believe in my heart it is desperately needed. When asked what he did for a living, one of my co-workers used to say, facetiously, "I write comedy and save lives!" I've stolen that as a slogan, but I'm not facetious about it because I know there is a place where magic abides. In my teen years, when I loathed myself in a way that makes Fred Phelps' hatred look like amateur night, it was the combined power of laugher, love, and theater that saved me.

That, Mr. Cutler, is why there are so many homosexuals in the theater. It's where we found ourselves.

Oh, and full disclosure: It's also where I found my awesome husband. What, like I was gonna look somewhere else?

∾

JOEL PERRY WROTE, *directed, and produced syndicated radio comedy for DJs across the US and Canada for twenty-four years. He was associate editor at Instinct Magazine, where he wrote the advice column for seventeen years. He has five books released, including the Lamda nominated* That's Why They're in Cages, People, *and a novel about Hollywood at its wonderful worst called* Stealing Arthur. *He also wrote* Azalea Festival Queen *that was recently directed by his husband at TheatreNOW in Wilmington, North Carolina.*

A RING OF TRUTH

K. ROBERT CAMPBELL

I t started the day I had to crawl under the house.

It's an old place, built in about 1903 or so. I live at the North Carolina coast and back then they usually built houses on short brick pilings to get them off the ground, leaving bare sand underneath. At some point, brick foundation walls were built under my house to keep the wind out. Sewer and water lines got put in, heat ducts and insulation got put in; by the time we bought it, everything was pretty well modernized.

I guess "modernized" is a relative term. I think sewer lines were laid under the house in the thirties. They used heavy cast-iron pipe for the main line to the street.

So, a couple months ago the sewer system started backing up. We called a plumber a couple of times. He'd run some kind of tool up the line from the street and it would clear things up for a while. But eventually, the system would clog again.

Sally, that's my wife, really got on my case the day the downstairs shower stall overflowed and poured water out all over the place. I don't know what was in that water, but it stunk like the dickens. Well, I do know what was in the water, but I wasn't about to tell her.

I'm fairly handy with tools. I used to help my dad with projects a lot when I was growing up. Sally never had much faith in my skills though. She was always telling me to "Call the man."

Now, this latest overflow was on a Sunday, so I wasn't about to pay weekend rates to a plumber. I said, "I can do this myself. Let's just wait until tomorrow when the hardware store opens. You can go over to your sister's house across town if you need a shower that bad."

She said, "You don't know anything about pipes. Just call the man or I'll call him for you."

That set me off and we wound up bickering the rest of the day. I finally told her if she called that plumber, she might as well pack her things and move in with her sister.

My plan was to crawl under the house on Monday to dig up the old pipe. I figured I'd be able to find out what was wrong once and for all and fix it.

Sally did pack up her things, but just one night's worth. She got fed up and told me, "You want to fix it, then fix it. But you better do it right. I'll be at my sister's house."

I told her, "Good, if it'll get you off my back." She slammed the door when she left.

First thing Monday morning I flushed the downstairs toilet to see if there was still a backup. It drained down a little slow but it didn't block up completely. I figured most of the backup must have trickled down the line overnight.

I grabbed a pickaxe and one of those folding army shovels out of the garage and headed under the house with a flashlight. The crawlspace is only about three feet high and there were a lot of wires and pipes hanging from the floor joists, so it took some maneuvering through the sand to get to the drain pipe furthest toward the back. All the while, I was thinking about how much Sally better appreciate all I was going through to save us some money.

When I finally got back to the drain pipe, I started digging the main sewer line out. At first, it was barely buried under the sand, but the further I got toward the front of the house, the deeper it got. I was throwing dirt left and right trying to get the job done. But when I tossed one shovelful past the flashlight beam, a glint of yellow happened to catch my eye. For some reason, I decided to take a break and see what it was.

After setting the flashlight in a better position, I sat up the best I could in my cramped quarters and started sifting through the sand. My back started hurting after a while and I was about to give up and get back to work. Suddenly, there it sat in the palm of my hand— an old gold ring shining in the dim light. The band was pretty plain, but the top was shaped like a dragon's head.

I brushed it off, shining the light all over it as I did. Inside the band were the initials "D. L." I was tired and thirsty anyway, so I squiggled back to the crawl space entryway. Outside in the sunlight, I stood and stretched before taking a closer look at the ring.

The dragon head had something set into it that was coated with dirt, so I couldn't tell what it was at first. Once I washed it off under the outside spigot, I saw that some kind of bright red stone served as the dragon's eye. I don't know what kind of gem it was but it almost seemed to have a glow of its own, even in the shade.

Just for the heck of it, I decided to try the ring on. I couldn't believe my luck; it was a perfect fit. Funny though, for a second or two it looked like the red stone glowed even a little brighter. I just figured the sun was hitting it at a different angle.

Right after the stone glowed brighter, I started to feel a little funny. Not dizzy, exactly. I can't really say what the feeling was. I just know I felt different, not...myself.

I'd worked up quite an appetite crawling around and

working under the house. It was about one o'clock anyway, so I broke for lunch.

While I was eating, Sally came home. She looked me up and down, saw how dirty I was and sneered, "I hope you got your little chore done, because you need to use the shower right now. Get your nasty self out of my kitchen and go clean up!"

I told her, "It took me all morning just to get the pipes dug up. I have to start breaking the old pipes loose so I can put new ones in now."

She said, "I'm not spending another night outside my home," and reached for the phone. I think the next thing she said was, "I don't care what it costs, I'm getting the plumber over here to do it right."

I say I think she said that because I was sort of listening to two people at the same time. I distinctly remember someone else saying, "You going to let a wench talk to you like that, mate?"

I looked over my shoulder to see who else was there but I didn't see anybody. When I looked back at Sally, she was staring at me, saying, "What did you say?"

I answered, "I didn't say anything. What are you talking about?"

She actually started laughing and asked, "Did you just call me a wench?"

I answered, "I didn't call you anything, but you heard that voice too?"

"Of course I heard that voice; it was yours. What kind of game are you trying to play?"

I thought it best to let things be and said, "Look, I don't feel too good. Go ahead and call your plumber if you think you have to. I'm going to go lay down."

She said, "Not until you take off those nasty clothes you won't."

I said, "Fine," as I huffed toward the stairway and got her out of my sight.

As I climbed the stairs, I heard her talking to the plumber on the phone.

By the time I got to the top of the stairs, the voice was back, saying, "Wouldn't put up with that from none of my wenches, mate. Wouldn't at all." I looked over my shoulder again but still saw no one. I thought, "Great, now I'm getting delusional."

I did change out of my dirty clothes and wash up a little before I hit the bed. Rest wouldn't come easily though. I kept thinking about the ring and who might have lost it. There was no telling when it might have got buried in the sand. Maybe it belonged to a long-ago owner of the house?

I must have drifted off for a little while, because I remember having some strange dreams about being on an old wooden ship. Everything was a little foggy but I remember that my shipmates looked pretty skuzzy.

After waking up, I tossed and turned for a while until I couldn't stand it any longer. I decided to do a little research and see if I could find out who originally owned that ring. I got up and walked downstairs.

Sally was still in the kitchen, drinking coffee. I heard thumps and bumps under the house and said, "I see you got hold of your plumber. Sure hope you can figure out how we're going to pay him."

She said, "Don't worry, I'll figure it out."

I told her, "'Long as I'm playing hooky from work anyway, I'm going out for a while."

"Out where?"

"Just out."

"That's fine, leave me stuck here with the plumber. Thanks a lot."

On the way out the door, I said, "You're very welcome. Why don't you crawl under the house and keep him company?"

As I climbed into the car, I got a sudden dizzy spell. I had to plop down hard and sit very still for a few moments before hitting the road.

I drove to the courthouse, where the real estate records are kept, figuring I might find a history of who owned my house over the years. The people at the register of deeds office were very helpful, giving me some pointers on how to trace the ownership records. In no time, I had a compilation of owners from the time the house was built until the time I bought it. None of them had the initials "D.L." though.

It was a little disappointing; I was sure some past owner of the house must have lost the ring there. I stood at one of the tall tables in the registry, staring blankly over the list of names I'd compiled. Suddenly, my eyes focused on the name of somebody who bought the house in 1939 and lived in it until 1945, when his mortgage was foreclosed.

As I looked at the name, Frederick Constantine, the voice came back. It said, "Aye, that was us," and started laughing. A woman standing on the other side of the table gave me a startled look and I asked, "Did you hear that too?" She closed the record book she had been studying and hurried to put it back on the shelf. I felt the vertigo coming on again and quickly sat on a nearby stool for a few moments.

For some reason the name Frederick Constantine struck a bell with me. I called my buddy John Stamper on my cell phone and asked if he ever heard of that name. John likes to dabble in local history, so I figured he'd know if anybody did.

When I asked him, John thought for a little bit before he answered. "You know, I think that was a guy who killed his wife back in the forties," he said. "Caused quite a stir at the time. What brings his name up?"

I told him, "According to the county records, the guy owned my house back in the forties. In fact, it got sold out from under him in '45 when his mortgage was foreclosed."

He said, "That would make sense. I think he killed his wife early that year. If memory serves me right, a jury found him insane and he got put in an asylum. I think he finally died some time in the early seventies. They didn't have any kids that I know of."

I asked, "Did you say they found him insane?"

He answered, "Yeah. I don't remember the details though. Why don't you check out the archives down at the paper?"

I thanked him and said I would check it out right away. The newspaper office wasn't that far from the courthouse and I got there in no time. The folks at the paper's archive department were very helpful and soon I zeroed in on the story of the Constantine murder. The headline was rather odd. It said, "Local Man Says Pirate Ordered Wife's Execution."

Intrigued, I read through the article. According to the reporter, "The defendant, Mr. Constantine, said he found a dragon-head ring under his house one day and it fit him perfectly. Constantine testified that shortly after he began wearing the ring, a voice started speaking in his head claiming to be the spirit of an old pirate named David Lassiter, a member of pirate captain Stede Bonnet's crew."

The article went on, "Bonnet was captured in the early 1700s, during a fierce ship battle near our county. He and his surviving crew were taken to Charleston, South Carolina, where they were tried, found guilty of piracy, and hung.

"The county prosecutor brought up the fact that Lassiter's name never appeared in any accounts of the hangings. Constantine's explanation: Lassiter claimed he jumped ship during the battle and thought he'd made a good escape until soldiers caught up with him, apparently at the location where our town now sits.

"According to Constantine, the Lassiter voice told him that he had ditched his distinctive ring just before he got caught, hoping it would make it harder for anyone to verify who he was. It didn't work—they recognized him anyway and tried to seize him. Lassiter started to run but they shot him in the back."

I looked around me when I heard someone say, "The dirty cowards." No one was near.

I read on, "Constantine told the jury that Lassiter's voice started talking to him more and more, and after a while, he started getting lapses of memory. He could not account for his activities or whereabouts for hours at a time. He tried to take off the ring, hoping the voices and lapses would stop, but it would not come off no matter how hard he tried."

About this point in my reading, I became conscious that I'd begun tugging at my new ring. It had gone on so easily, I didn't think there would be much problem getting it off. It wouldn't budge; as if my knuckle got swollen unexpectedly.

I decided I'd finish reading the article and then go home and put some salad oil or something on my finger so I could get the ring off.

The account continued, "Constantine and his wife Ernestine weren't getting along very well and she got increasingly angry about his unexplained absences. One night, Mrs. Constantine found a secret hiding place in the house that was filled with valuables. She'd been reading about break-ins around town put two-and-two together. She told Fred she was calling the police.

"Constantine claimed that when his wife threatened to turn him in, the voice in his head said, 'Don't let her do it, mate. We ain't goin' that easy, not again.' The next thing he knew, he went blank again. Hours later, he found himself sitting in his living room staring at the walls. Someone was pounding on his front door and he got up to answer it. When he reached for the doorknob, he noticed that his hands were coated with dirt and dust and his right ring finger was bloodied and bare. His clothes were filthy as well.

"When Constantine opened the door, he found himself facing the local police. Apparently some neighbors heard screaming earlier in the evening and the police were checking the neighborhood to see if everyone was all right. He stared blankly at the policemen for a moment and when they saw how dirty he was, they asked where his wife was. He had no answer and they grew especially suspicious on spying the bloody ring finger.

"The police searched and found Mrs. Constantine buried under the house, her head bashed in by the same shovel that was used to bury her.

"Constantine's defense was built on his insistence that he was taken over by evil spirits. His defense attorney brought in expert witnesses to attest to his belief in those spirits and it won him the insanity verdict. Constantine still insists he never knew how his wife came to be killed and that it was all connected to the ring. Oddly enough, no one ever found the missing ring. The prosecutor told that jury that Constantine made up the story after he banged his finger while burying his wife."

I was astounded by the story. I even thought I might be able to vindicate poor Mr. Constantine after all these years. Before I closed the archive book, I thought I heard someone laughing over my shoulder. I turned around to look but nobody was there. Some reporters were talking in a nearby office and I decided it must have been one of them.

By this time, it was close to five, so I went home. Sally was still there, fuming because I'd been gone so long. I think I must have blanked out for a few seconds because I don't remember saying anything to her, but the next thing I knew, she was looking at me kind of scared-like. She didn't say anything to me and just started setting out supper. We didn't talk at all while we ate so I excused myself right after supper and went upstairs. I went into the bathroom, found some of Sally's hand cream, and smeared it on my ring finger. I tugged and pulled at the ring, but it still wouldn't come off.

Just then, Sally came up the stairs. She stood in the bathroom doorway and asked, "What's the matter with you? You're acting weird. You've gone off who knows where instead of going to work today and...where did that ring come from?"

I looked at my finger self-consciously, saying nothing, but I was aware of a strange feeling welling up inside me.

Sally said, "If you ever threaten me again like you did downstairs just now, I'm going straight to the police, you understand?"

I said, "I have no idea what you're talking about. I've never threatened you."

Her voice rose. "I can't believe you'd say the things you just said to me and then stand here and deny it. Have you lost your mind?"

The voice was behind me again. It said, "Don't let her push you. She needs a good whipping."

Sally's eyes widened and she said, "That's it! I told you not to threaten me again and I meant it. I'm calling the police right now." She wheeled around and headed down the hall toward our bedroom. I felt my face flush and then I went blank.

I came to, several hours later, sitting on the living room couch and breathing heavily. Someone was pounding on the door. It was the police, of course. I have no recollection of what happened between the time Sally stomped down the hall and the time I heard the pounding.

I've been told that the police found Sally's body buried in the sand under the house and that her head had been bashed in by my foldable shovel. I don't have any idea how that happened so I can't admit or deny whether I did it. I do recall that the police were able to remove the ring from my finger pretty easily when I was being processed into the jail.

Well, that's how all this came about and why I'm sitting here talking to all of you today. I know it's hard to believe, but it's the only explanation I've got.

~

No one in the courtroom said a word. Some of the jurors gave each other sidelong glances, perhaps to determine if any one of them believed the story they just heard. Eventually, defense attorney Hoskins stood and said, "We rest our case, Your Honor."

Judge Schultz raised one eyebrow and said, "No more evidence for the defense?"

"No, Your Honor."

He looked at prosecutor Eldridge and asked, "Any cross-examination?"

Eldridge smiled smugly and said, "Don't believe any is needed, Your Honor."

The defendant went back to the defense table. Judge Schultz excused the jurors and after they were safely sequestered, he asked Hoskins, "Are you not going to produce any more evidence than the story your client just told?"

Hoskins responded, "Your Honor, my client insisted that I present his defense exactly as I've done it. Of course, I'm asking for a verdict of not guilty by reason of insanity."

"But you've presented no medical experts to back that claim. The only thing you've done is allow your client to tell his ridiculous tale."

"Nevertheless, Your Honor, I've done as my client wished. I've counseled and warned him and this is what he wanted."

Judge Schultz looked at the defendant and instructed him to stand. He asked, "Is this true, what your lawyer just told me?"

The defendant responded, "Yes, sir, that's what I want. Everything happened just like I said and I wanted the jury to know. I let my lawyer try the insanity defense against my better judgment."

"You understand that if the jury finds you guilty, you will be convicted of a capital offense and may get the death sentence?"

"Yes, Your Honor. I understand. I know the doctors say there's nothing wrong with me and I agree with them; there isn't anything wrong with me. What I said here today is the truth and nothing but the truth, so help me God."

With a sigh, Judge Schultz told the bailiff to bring the jury back. When they were seated, he told prosecutor Eldridge, "They're all yours."

Eldridge rose from his table, took a dramatic pause, and began addressing the jury.

"Ladies and gentlemen of the jury," he began, "I wish you would join me in a round of applause for the defendant. He just told us an entertaining story." He clapped, but none of the jurors joined him. He didn't expect them to.

He continued, "I used to listen to ghost stories when I

was a kid. Found them very scary in fact. But what scares me more is the thought that you might believe that man's story and let him walk free."

Eldridge walked over to the jury box and leaned on the rail. He pointed to Hoskins and said, "My esteemed colleague over there will soon attempt to talk you into declaring his client not guilty by reason of insanity. You will have to decide whether to let him get away with such nonsense. I submit to you that once you've reviewed all the evidence, you'll agree with me that this defendant has committed nothing but cold-blooded murder. He had the motive and he had the opportunity and he knew exactly what he was doing. There's no reasonable doubt about it."

He smiled for a second; a carefully timed smile, carefully practiced in front of a mirror only hours earlier. "I'll admit; it was a good story. Sounds almost plausible if you don't think about it too hard." He waited for a carefully timed moment before walking a few steps away from the jury box. He wanted the jury to think about it too hard.

"I hope you'll really think about how conveniently his story parallels the Constantine murder case. Man finds mysterious ring under house. Man tries ring on; a perfect fit until he tries to remove it. Man starts hearing 'voices' and having blackouts. Sounds too familiar, doesn't it?"

Some of the jurors nodded in agreement. Exactly what he was hoping for.

"Yes, ladies and gentlemen, this 'ghost pirate' is what made him do it. Never mind the State's evidence to the contrary, it was the ghost.' He allowed himself a little derisive snort.

"Let's examine the State's evidence, shall we? You

heard three doctors—three—testify that they examined the defendant. You heard their credentials. They are all highly trained experts in psychiatry. Not one of them found any sign of mental illness in this defendant. You heard them say that aside from a predisposition to story-telling dating back to his childhood, the defendant had never shown any sign of mental abnormality that they could discern."

Eldridge was warming up. "You heard from no less than six friends of the defendant and his wife. And what did they all tell you? The defendant and his wife had been at odds with each other for months. They argued about everything, loudly and anywhere. He threatened her life on more than one occasion. Their friends found it all quite embarrassing, even frightening. Motive, my friends, motive. He was tired of his wife and wanted her out of the way."

He paced in front of the jury box for a couple of turns. "The police. What did you hear from the police? They got some calls—people heard what sounded like a woman screaming. No one could pinpoint the source of the sound, so the police waited. You heard Officer McMullens say that people weren't even sure whether it might have been neighborhood kids screeching.

"Then the one call came in. You remember, the reluc-tant neighbor, the one who thought she might get in trou-ble? She lives right next door to the defendant and has heard he and his wife screeching at each other before. She called the police before but Sally would always deny that anything was wrong. But this time it sounded differ-ent, didn't it? She told you that this time, Sally sounded more, how did she say it, 'desperate.' And then everything went silent. The only voices she heard before that were the defendant and his wife." With a sneer, he added, "No 'pirates,' nobody else." He paused for the jury to absorb his 'pirate' comment and then continued, "She debated what to do for hours before deciding to do the right thing and calling the police.

"And what did the police find when they went to the defendant's house? They found him, dirty and disheveled, with blood on his shirt. He claimed he didn't know where Sally was. We know where she was though, don't we? She was right under his feet, under the house, where he just buried her! And what did he have the nerve to do? He blamed the whole thing on the voices in his head and made up some story about pirate spirits."

Eldridge stopped and rubbed his chin before saying, "You might have noticed that the defendant has neither confirmed nor denied that he killed his wife. He had every right to say nothing at all, but he chose to go up to that stand, be put under oath and tell you his version of what happened. It's up to you to decide whether he violated that oath, but I'll ask you to look at all the evidence—the doctors, the neighbors, the forensic experts—and then come back here and tell me that you believe what that man has said."

Eldridge wanted to add one more flourish before he was through. He walked to the evidence table and picked up the dragon-head ring. Holding it in the air, he said, "Members of the jury, the defendant would have you believe that some mysterious spirit entered his body when he first slipped this ring onto his finger. He would have you believe that this spirit took him over and directed him to execute his wife.

"I submit to you, ladies and gentlemen, that the defendant's story is true up to the point that he found this ring under his house. But I will also submit that he told the story backwards from there on; he did all his research first and found the perfect story to cover the cold-blooded murder he planned to commit. He would reenact a murder from more than half a century ago and blame it all on this so-called pirate's ring.

Eldridge held the ring over his right-hand ring finger before concluding, "And I finally submit to you, members of the jury, that his story does not 'ring' true." He then slipped the ring onto his finger with a flair.

This final touch had the expected effect. The jurors were his and he knew it. Most of them grinned and nodded when he put the ring on his finger. He smiled confidently to himself when he turned to go back to his table. Suddenly he paused for a moment and stared down at the ring. Just as suddenly, he turned and looked questioningly at the judge, as if His Honor had just said something. Judge Schultz simply stared blankly back at him.

Eldridge shook his head and sat down. He tried to remove the ring so he could return it to the evidence table, in case Hoskins wanted to use it in his arguments. It would not come off. He put his hands under the table and worked it some more with the same result. He gave up for the time being and hoped no one would notice he still had it on.

Hoskins gave it his best, but he could not persuade the jury. They found the defendant guilty and gave him the death sentence.

Word about the "Pirate Murder" spread fast. People

laughed as they congratulated Eldridge on his clever closing argument. The laughs came to a sudden halt two weeks later, on the day that headlines rang out: "Prosecutor Eldridge Kills Two In Unprovoked Attack: Blames Pirate Ghost."

~

KENNETH CAMPBELL is the author of the Cameron Scott suspense series, which is set in Southeast North Carolina, beginning with The Fifth Category, *and working downward through* The Fourth Estate, The Third Degree, Second Hand, *and* First Class. *He has been active in Brunswick and New Hanover County theater, and his comedy* Radio Play *and musical* Winter Nightson *were produced in Brunswick County.*

8 MINUTES, 20 SECONDS

JOSH BAILEY

She sat on her chair alone in the middle of the intersection with her cardboard sign, oblivious, or perhaps all too aware of the running, screaming people around her or of the honking cars behind. Her ten-year-old, Pippy-Longstockinged head, complete with pigtails and freckles, held a lilting, malevolent grin only contested by the sign in her grasp:

"Repent now all ye mother----!"

I moved along, crossed the intersection, and felt her glowing blue eyes burn predatorily into my back. I wondered about the lonely evangelist. Perhaps: where were her parents? Why was she so calm when the whole rest of the world was insane? Or maybe it was only her.

The road I turned along was barren of people, but they had left their mark quickly and efficiently. Where once I had walked crossing paths with street vendors and tourists, corner divas and nickel musicians, junkie poets and famished fashionistas, now trash and broken glass littered the ground. The stores I once shopped in, spending money on things I didn't need or on gifts for people I didn't know, laid broken and looted unless they were boarded up, and even then they usually suffered the same fate. Every ground-story window was shattered, and here or there small pools of blood hinted at dark deeds that now moldered in the back alleys awaiting a discovery that, here, at the end, would never come.

The coffee shop on the corner, once packed with caffeine-addled coffee connoisseurs from the opening chime to the closing lock, ironically enough, was unscathed. As I crossed the street, my reflection materialized in the large, store-front window and moved towards me. Stepping cautiously up over the curb, we met, my hand extending as he did the same and we silently touched, the ice of the window separating our two worlds by a mere fraction of disjointed space. Peering into his eyes for a moment I saw his life flash by and wondered if he saw the same in me. I waited for his answer, but was thankful when he remained silent, not wanting my imminent death to be so clichély foretold. Something beyond him caught my eye, and I focused into the store, banishing him forever away from my mind and from existence, and that's when I saw her.

For the past four hours I had been alone. I left my mother's apartment with assurances that the end of the would come; that she would spend her remaining day, maybe two, praying with hands clasped, eyes towards heaven, fasting and waiting for some untold light to beam her up, Scottie, or some chariot of fire to whisk her to heaven or Valhalla or wherever her fare would take her. I headed down the block, across 34th street, up to Stone Haven, through the blue door with the brass knocker, nodded at Lady Lauren, the old maid, felt beneath his welcome mat for the ill-hidden key, and entered my father's two-bedroom, one-bath apartment. He wasn't there, which meant he now sat at the corner in Shanahan's Pub doing his final days of prayer the only way he knew how: with a steady, cold river of the finest ale on tap, hands clasped around the largest pint, eyes raised towards the plasma screen. I didn't go to find him.

Wanting neither to pray nor drink myself into a stupor—not wanting to be drunk in either way when the end finally came—I walked and walked through the living city that slowly belabored its dying breath, and oh, what a breath it was. The clogged arteries of the main roads, where those who thought running would save them from doom drove their cars to their stops, had been abandoned long ago as the Exodus out of the heart towards the extremities began, yet I trekked down them finding my way deeper towards the core: to Central Park and the zoo and the tiger.

In their cages they were screaming and yelling, and it reminded me of the day I left Osaka and traveled in to Tokyo when the earthquake hit and all the dogs ran in the streets baying at the dumb humans to abandon ship. Or when all the birds in the city took off at once, crowing out alarm bells that rang too silently for self-occupied human ears to hear. In the city streets the rats came out of the sewers in droves and ran in the gutters and across the fallen refuse, frightening pedestrians but not enough to question the rats' presence. When the first tremor hit we ducked and braced, and when the calm came we sighed relief, and only days later did anyone comment on the odd behavior of the animals.

When I came to the tiger cage, he was lying calmly where he had once laid fifteen years before, but I viewed this with much older eyes. I remember the air being tinted with cotton candy and bubble gum then, and the sun was a lemon drop and the greatest threat to my existence was a tumble over the railing into the lions' pit, not the destruction of the world. A balloon that looked like a giraffe was tied around the wrist of the hand that clutched tightly to the hem of my mother's skirt. My eyes, filled with joy, gazed out at the tiger laying in the mottled sunlight, and I could feel his cold stare on me just as I could feel my mother's eyes on me. This came before hers were clouded with tears, before the split, and somewhere in the corner of my vision dad snapped photographs and laughed, and he was sober.

The balloon tethered to my arm was ripped away with a gust and the cotton candy air tinged with grief and sadness and fifteen years was past and I was standing in the same spot, much less green, but still with the same eyes that looked at the tiger. The lilt of his tail hinted at his calmness as it swung slowly back and forth, like the metronome to a fugue. In the cage next to him a panther was attempting to climb up the fence, leaping from it to a tree and back again, mewling like some kind of demon trapped on the wrong side of St. Peter's gate. Across the way a lion was attempting to keep his entire pride off his rock, apparently thinking it would be the one safe place on earth and he was making it alone. The sea of action all around crashed idly against the stoic rock of the tiger and moved him not.

When I finally lifted my eyes to his, they pierced me through, and their deep ice was like the window and in him I saw my reflection, and this time my life flashed before my eyes. From childhood through preschool to growth spurts and awkward teenage years, to first kisses, first dates, college, dropping out, and returning to finally graduate, I saw it all until today and then back again. Once more I was in the cotton candy air with the tiger and those piercing eyes and that lilting tail, and then I was in front of the café window and all the past washed out, its flotsam and jetsam floundering on the beach of the present to reveal those same piercing eyes except in human form, filtered through the ice of the window and my discarded reflection. Her.

Leaving Central Park, a man attempted to mug me

but thought better when he saw my size in relation to his and resorted to apologizing profusely. "You just know how the times are, man." I nodded. "They're too short." I nodded again. "I just, I just...want'a feel rich for once before I die and they say tomorrow, or the next day, whenever it goes, we've only got 8 minutes and 20 seconds. We won't know either. It'll just happen and we'll live those next 8 minutes and 20 seconds after it does and then we'll be gone." He snapped for emphasis, "and I just want to feel rich once, even if it is only for less than ten minutes."

I emptied my pockets and filled his, although it wasn't much and it sure wasn't "rich" by any standards. His reason for wanting money was just as good as any, but now that I looked over the menu in the vacant coffee shop I wish I had $3.40 for a latte. I could buy an excuse then to stop staring through the window and enter in, wait at the counter for a minute with those eyes staring. They stared now, the ice of the window separating us, until finally I turned to the door and entered the abandoned shop.

"I'm afraid there's nothing to drink." She was sipping on water, her gaze out the window and not towards me as I had hoped. Her voice carried a vaguely British air, but the kind that had long been mellowed by years in the former colony. Nodding towards her water she added, "I suppose unless you want water." Which I did, since she suggested it.

I went behind the counter, picked a cardboard cup out of its holder, placed it under the tap, and filled it to the brim with cold water. Taking a drink I realized how thirsty I was after walking all day, and I went back around the counter where finally she had turned her attention from the empty street to me. "You're an odd bird."

I smiled and drank, and she continued, "Everyone else is migrating away from here, and you've stayed behind." She sipped and I sipped and she continued, "I guess if you were staying for me it would be chivalrous."

"I could be."

"You don't know me."

"I could."

She sipped and I sipped, and then she smiled. "Perhaps." With her free hand she motioned to the other seat at her table, and I took it.

"Thank you."

"I suppose you've nowhere else to sit." She looked around, crowding the café with her imagination, and smiled. "Make yourself at home."

I eyed her for a moment, sizing up her self-assured aura, piercing eyes, unassuming, yet all-too-prevalent beauty, and then spoke. "I suppose we flock together."

She nodded, leaned towards me and whispered as if to hide her words from listening ears, "Birds of a feather." Her blue eyes were following the movement of my hand from table to cup to mouth and back, apparently sizing me up as well, "Are we crazy?"

I answered suddenly, unsure if it was the right answer for the play or not, "Yes."

"And no." She smiled. "Because aren't they all crazy to run?"

"If we're doomed anyway, I suppose running just wastes time."

"And we've got so little."

For a moment I lowered my eyes, attempting to hide

the grief in my eyes. My mother was alone in her apartment, most likely at the foot of her bed, her hands clasped together. Thinking of her there, her life ending in flames with no one to share in the ash, it pained me.

"But for all we know we've got so much." I couldn't tell if she was attempting to reassure me or not.

"Eight minutes, I'm told."

"And twenty seconds. Don't forget that." She turned towards me, her hand reaching out and resting on mine. "It's all the time in the world."

I looked down at her perfectly manicured hand, barren of any rings—on a finger that mattered, at least—and then slowly up to her face. It was warm, yet calculating, and with the ice blue eyes, two contrasting elements yinged and yanged around to form something very unfamiliar. "Who are you?"

After a moment she finally broke the gaze and looked back outside, taking the last sip of her water. "I'm me."

I sighed. "Me too."

"I guess that saves us introductions." Her finger was drawing circles on the tabletop, lilting in ellipses like the orbit of the earth around its dangerous sun. We sat in silence for a moment, and when my cup had emptied and filled both of ours again from the tap. When I sat hers down in front of her, she reached out and grabbed my wrist. "What time is it?" I looked at my watch, then questioningly at her. "Yes, the time please." She waved me on.

"6:30." I raised an eyebrow as if to question, "Does it matter?"

"Of course it matters! It's supper time, and it always matters." She quickly drank her water and motioned for me. "Drink up."

I did, the cold water washing down my throat, chilling my body as it went. Moments later I felt the icy touch in my head as the chill shocked my nerves into pain.

"Are you hungry?"

I nodded, realizing that I hadn't had anything to eat all day. "Actually, I'm famished."

"Good word." The corner of her mouth lifted as she bit idly at one of her nails. She pulled it out of her mouth suddenly and attempted to smooth it out with another finger as if to scold herself for ruining the manicure. Finally, she reached out, took my hand, stood up, and began to pull me towards the door.

"Where are we going?" I looked out at the empty street where the only sign of life was a dog scurrying mindlessly from one side of the road to the other. I couldn't imagine where or what we'd be eating that night.

"My place of course." She dragged me on, and the quickly stopped, turned around, and placed a few dollars on the table. "Forgot to pay." And off we were again.

Dinner was a chicken sandwich with macaroni and cheese and a piece of birthday cake. "It's not mine." She assured me as we blew out a candle she'd insisted be lit on top.

"What are we celebrating?"

"The end." We blew together. "Or...a beginning. You never can tell these days, and often the two seem to be the exact same thing."

We walked out onto her balcony which overlooked the higher numbered streets, and as far as we could see cars had been abandoned on the roads. In the distance, the lights on the bridge were just coming up, yet we could see the slowly moving traffic that was flowing out of the city. I couldn't see how they thought leaving the city would save them, but maybe I was wrong and it would only hit here. The destruction of the world would only be mine, and the rest of Earth would be left unscathed. My tiny corner of Earth—my world: my mom and her prayers, my dad and his pub, this woman and her apartment, Central Park and the tiger—would be gone come dawn, but the suburbs, the sprawl, America, the world as a whole, would all be here, breathe a sigh of relief and release a prayer for those who'd stayed stupidly behind in the city that was no more. For a moment she disappeared inside and the wind rising up off the streets, racing up and between the skyscrapers blew into my face, bringing with it the smell of this place I called home, and, from somewhere far-off, the smell of trees and flowers and life.

She returned with two champagne flutes in her hand, each bubbling over with the translucent beverage. "Cheers," she said, handing me a glass.

"More celebrating."

"No, I'm just trying to get you drunk."

I met her gaze. She wasn't joking. Laughing, I clinked my glass against hers and took a sip, the fizz popping and splashing against my mouth and nose. Bringing the drink down, I realized that she was there, and the city was coming to life around us as the automated lights along the streets and on the buildings blinked on as the sun blinked down below the horizon. Another gust of wind shot up from the street, bringing the warmth of the day stored there up to us, and I leaned in for a first kiss with a woman I didn't know, with a name I hadn't learned, but with the world ending it seemed like the right time.

After a moment she pulled back, licked her lips and

smiled. "Spot on." She took a sip of her champagne, placed a hand on the railing and leaned over, staring out across the city. Suddenly, her laughter rang out and echoed back from every corner and the wind rushed carrying it up, up, and out away from us to those fleeing drivers and pedestrians. She turned to me, placed a hand in mine, her smile spread from ear to ear, and her ice blue eyes with a look like a predator eyeing prey. It wasn't a frightening look, though, but a welcome one. One I'd been waiting on for years, had known was coming, had wanted to come, and when it finally arrived I surrendered to it. "Let's get married." The words were quickly out of her mouth, like a creek gushing out of a mountain filled with Spring melt water.

Again, without thinking or without needing to think, I answered, "Yes."

"And have three children, and live in some stuffy suburban neighborhood, and send them to a private school where all the other parents talk badly about us behind our backs because we're the couple from the city."

I kissed her again and planned our entire future together with just one more word,

"Anything." As long as it was with her.

One final flash of sunlight was bouncing off of the low clouds on the horizon, sending bright purple and red flares out across the sky as warning beacons of the morrow, and what would come then. The scientists said, "Tomorrow, or the next day," but the whole world knew, and we knew standing alone on the balcony, our whole future planned out with one kiss and one word. Tomorrow.

∿

WE SLEPT that night on top of the quilt her grandmother had made for her before she'd come to the city for college and never gone home. I'd pulled my shoes off and we laid together as a double-"S," me whispering in her ear, my hand on her stomach feeling the distant rise and fall of her diaphragm as it pushed laughter and smiles up from her base. At 4:30 that morning I learned that her name was Katherine, but it didn't change anything. At 5:00 I gave her a Cheerio engagement ring and we put our shoes on and rushed out onto the abandoned streets, the lamps on the corners encircling us in hugs of light where we kissed until I realized what day it was and that it was the last.

"It's tomorrow already."

"It is." And she laughed and kissed me, and we celebrated the end.

Stopping, I thought of my mother and father, and knew he was passed out on his couch with the TV on, although now it would be nothing but bars and the monotone, and my mother would be asleep if she still wasn't praying. I looked into her eyes, those piercing eyes, and at her lilting smile and I knew. "Let's go to the zoo."

"The zoo?"

"Central Park."

She cocked her head to the side, analyzing me for a moment, and then said, "Perfect place for a honeymoon. Let's go to the zoo."

We walked, and before we knew, we were there. We passed the lake where once I had sat for hours and wondered at the words of Holden Caulfield about the

ducks in winter, and finally we made our way to the zoo
where there were no people, but the animals were still all
there, caged for their final bout with planet Earth.

As we reached the tiger cage, the first rays of the sun
were peeking over the horizon, splashing against the
trees of the park, glinting off the far-off rooftops, and
heralding the new day. The lion across the way let out a
fearsome yawn, and opened one eye to make sure he had
successfully defended his rock through the night, which
he had. The panther next to the tiger had given up
climbing the fence and was asleep in a tree, his paw
placed over his eye willing the dawning sun to sleep for
just a few minutes longer.

Alone in his cage, however, the tiger waited and
stared. When I saw him I knew he had been waiting for
my return and I smiled. His tail was swinging back and
forth, lilting to the funeral march of the planet, and his
eyes opened out to the world, unblinking. Seeing us, he
licked his mouth, his sharp teeth flashing in the dawn
light, and in him I saw a look of predatory hunger that
was not disquieting because I felt I had seen it somewhere before.

"I suppose this is it." She was staring at the tiger, and
he at her, and she was speaking to me and to him.

Taking her in my arms I kissed her cheek. "Yes."

"They were right after all."

"Yes."

"Tomorrow"

"Or the next day."

She looked at me, her eyes sad for the first time since
I met her. "No...tomorrow."

And then the tears came because I knew, "Today."

She buried her head in my chest and I felt her sobs rise up through my body until I was sobbing in time with her, and finally the tiger rose from his perch and began to pace around his cage. Somewhere in the city a great sound arose like the rustling of a forest during an autumn windstorm, and moments later a great cloud of birds rose up all around us and flew as one towards the ocean. As the birds stormed overhead, their calls awakened every dog in the city, and suddenly we were no longer alone as the howls and yips of hundreds, if not thousands of dogs followed the retreating birds into the dawn light.

Suddenly, on the horizon the sun made itself known, bold and bright like a nuclear lemon drop. The air tinted with stale cotton candy and over-chewed bubble gum, and I kissed her deeply, holding her body close to mine, melding into one being.

All was light, but we felt the end before it came. Twenty seconds later all was dark.

But it was all the time in the world.

～

JOSH BAILEY is COLORADO BORN, Kentucky raised, and a current resident of Wilmington, NC. He spends the majority of his time as a professional educator, but dedicates much of his remaining energy to the arts. As an active member of the Wilmington theater community, he has acted in or directed over 25 plays, and his original plays, the one act A Good Old Fashioned Séance *and the full-length,* Greedy, *were produced at the Browncoat Theatre during the 2015-2016 season.*

JOHN WILLIS HOSTLER

SKIP MALONEY

The changes had always been subtle. He'd had no way of even noticing them when they began, nearly 4,000 years ago. But like senior citizens, as changes progressed, an awareness of mortality, which, for him, was hypothetical at best, did have a way of making him notice a few things.

Hearing seemed to be down a bit from its early stages of hypersensitivity to stimuli in his physical environment. Vision was growing more acute, as the eyes figuratively opened wider to embrace a broader range of visual experiences. He often tried to imagine how a man, born into a pre-civilization era, would have acted had someone lifted him from the European plains and dropped him into a 21st century, 3-D, IMAX theater in the middle of Manhattan. He imagined a heart attack; too much stimulation, overloading primitive circuitry.

Of course, he was, in a way, a pre-civilization man himself. He'd just had centuries and centuries to absorb the changes, gradually. By the time he sat down to a 3-D IMAX movie for the first time, he'd been through a number of eras, each with its own developing senses, and the reality they created for each and every individual on the planet.

You'd have thought that such longevity would have yielded him a rich tapestry of friends over the years, yet because of the need for isolation during some of the more dramatic periods of change, he'd been a loner all of his long, arguably over-extended lifetime. This had become particularly acute as modern man appeared on the stage, some 250,000 years ago. It took a while for this "modern man" to get his act together; to coalesce in various parts of the world and start contributing to what would eventually be known as civilization.

At first, nobody noticed when he disappeared for a period of time anywhere between a week and a year, and returned, literally, a different person. But as civilization started picking up speed, people around him became more aware of his comings and goings, and he'd not only shift biologically, he'd had to move, geographically.

The period between changes expanded and contracted on a timetable, unknowable to him. On average, he would age normally for about 20 years, but right around the time that his current list of friends and acquaintances would start showing their age, he would shift. He didn't regress 20 years, starting over. Something in him shifted subtly, and though he would continue to age, he did so at a remarkably, and permanently altered pace.

Each change, however, did age him, and though his body seemed to be adjusting to each shift, he was also aware that like the normal humans around him, there had to be a shelf life. He was tortured both by his awareness of how much time was likely left to him, and by an urgency to get there.

He was tired. Bone, marrow, and soul.

If asked, and of course, not being aware of his circumstances, no one ever did, he would likely tell you that this "millions of years of life" thing was more of a pain in the ass than a blessing. It just went on, and on, and on. He was not aware of anyone like him, although he had a way of cocking his head sideways to look at people he suspected had lived as long as he had. No one ever confirmed it. Any more than he did.

Lonely life.

On the other hand, there were some very acceptable fringe benefits. There were superficial things like the acquisition of wealth over the years. Like everybody else, he'd joined the working world when it became available, and figuratively, had banked hundreds of treasures, pensions among them, which resided, in one form or another, in banks all over the world. Nobody would be turning down his American Express card any time soon. He owned property in Rome, Berlin, Moscow, Japan and China, a by-product of his recurring need to occasionally be somewhere else for a while.

He was physically fit, and rarely sick. He could wake up on a Monday morning, after a hefty weekend of carousing, and run a marathon. Likely win it, too. While his body underwent more fundamental chemical changes slowly, he could adapt to changing circumstances rapidly. On that mean old Monday morning, once the starting gun went off to start that marathon, his body would catch on quickly, battling to overcome any vestiges of alcohol and fatigue, and immediately start gearing up.

OK, here we go... a marathon... system needs more blood flow, more oxygen... Check! And we're off...

John Willis Hostler hated running, so that sort of thing never cropped up.

He had an eerie sort of speed to him, though, and when it was necessary, he could call it up on demand. He became aware of it sometime in the 16th century. He'd been in a village somewhere in Europe (his memory had stopped storing insignificant information, like village names, thousands of years ago). One afternoon, this wagon got away from a horse that was

climbing up a hill, pulling it. The wagon, full of goods
on their way to a distant market, came barreling down
the hill, just as a toddler was stepping out onto the dirt
road. Hostler hadn't even looked around to see if
anybody was watching, a normal part of his procedure
when he was about to do something that might startle a
neighbor or two. He'd just moved. Real fast. Snatched
the kid out of the way into the tall grass to the side of the
road.

Someone had been watching, and was duly startled.
Limited intelligence, though, wouldn't allow the handful
of people who'd seen him run and grab the boy to realize
that what he'd just done was not, under normal circumstances, physically possible. They just marveled at how
quickly Hostler (Gabriel Jacobsen to them) had saved the
boy and they moved on.

He had strength and stamina way beyond the norm,
which, for a while (too long in his estimation) had
attracted the world's various armed forces. He'd been a
soldier off and on for nearly 200 years, before he got frustrated enough with the excuses people made to wage war
to quit altogether. His evolving body showed signs of the
fact that while he had certain indestructible qualities, a
bullet was capable of bringing him down. He had killed
enough. Had damn near been killed, quite a few times.
He was through with it.

Until... that morning in late February, as he walked
alone on North Carolina's Outer Banks, and saw the
woman running for her life. He didn't know this, at first,
of course. She'd just been a woman running. Looking a
little awkward as her equilibrium faced off against beach
sand. White shorts and blue halter top. Blond hair, whip-

ping in the wind, as she maintained forward motion, with regular looks over her shoulder.

Hostler's gaze shifted beyond her and saw the figure behind her, a couple of hundred yards away still, but gaining, and with what looked to be an automatic weapon. And then she saw Hostler and started to scream, angling her continually off-balance, forward-moving body in his direction. He looked around, at first, not because he was unsure of who she was screaming at, but as that precursor to decisive and potentially startling action.

Two objectives, he thought, analyzing quickly.

Do something with the woman!

Stop the man with the gun!

Woman first, but in order to accomplish both objectives, he needed them both just a shade or two closer. So he stood there, and let the woman get closer, now screaming words.

"Please!" she said, modulating her tone just enough to form the words. "Help me."

She had more to say, but her body was trying to make up its mind whether to supply her more oxygen for a speech, or maintain its attempt to get her the hell out of Dodge.

Tough decision.

Hostler closed the gap between them by a few steps and let her launch herself at him, forcing him to react. He caught her under the arms as she flailed and threw her over a dune to his left. He figured that he'd have some explaining to do about how he'd managed that, but first things first... the guy with the gun.

He'd stopped moving now, and he could tell from the

way the gunman had slowed, still a hundred or so yards off, that the man was trying to figure out what had just happened. Hostler still wasn't sure that the man was, in fact, trying to kill the woman. For all he knew, the man was a cop and the woman, a wanted murderer. Either way, though, he wasn't going to let the man approaching him shoot anybody. Not today. Not while he was on the beach.

He'd be forced to move if the guy brought the gun up and showed any signs of aiming it at him. He was hoping the guy would get a lot closer before that happened, and step by step, that was happening. And the guy was slowing down, his raised eyebrows and puzzled expression letting Hostler know that he was proceeding with caution at this man on the beach, standing stock still, who had just apparently thrown a woman about 100 feet away, with no more effort than if she'd been an apple.

The man came to full stop about 50 yards away, and looked around, assessing activity on the beach, which at this hour of the morning, was minimal. Hostler watched the action behind the man's eyes, and knew a second before the man did himself, that the semi-automatic weapon was on its way up for an alignment with Hostler's chest. And Hostler moved.

He was at the man's side before the man had time to react, and snatched the weapon out of the man's hands. If the man hadn't moved, Hostler would have left it at that. Just walked away. But the guy made an immediate and foolish attempt to get the weapon back, and Hostler clocked him. Slammed the butt end of the thing right at the guy's nose, and put him down. Still breathing, moaning, but not in the mood to do much else.

Hostler walked away, the weapon held loosely in his right hand, over to the dune, where the woman was on her hands and knees. She'd been watching.

"Who are you?" she asked, incredulous, right on the intelligence verge of understanding that she'd just witnessed something highly unusual, and in the world she'd come to know, likely impossible.

"My name's John Willis Hostler," he said. "I'm kind of new around here."

~

SKIP MALONEY WASN'T BORN in the South, but as he notes occasionally, he got there as soon as he could. Originally from Boston, and following a fifteen year hiatus in the NYC area, he now lives in Wilmington, NC. He is a staff writer for the AZBilliards web site, and does occasional freelance work for the national magazine Billiards Digest. He's an active member of Wilmington's theater community as a playwright, actor, director, and occasional producer. In his spare time, he's a tabletop boardgamer and occasional representative of Rio Grande Games at the annual World Boardgaming Championships.

POTTY STOP PERILS OR THE TRIALS AND TRIBULATIONS OF PUBLIC RESTROOMS

CHARLOTTE HACKMAN

Bathroom humor can take on many different connotations. In the literal explanation of bathroom humor, my endeavors were not explicitly connected with bodily functions, but rather incidents that took place in the bathroom. Specifically, I had two encounters in public restrooms, both while traveling. It isn't encouraging for an older woman with tiny bladder issues like me.

Men have an advantage in that they can usually find a tree to use or stand behind the open door of their car, pee and get away with it, or even an open door of the car opposite the traffic to relieve themselves when traveling. It's difficult for most women to do that...so we are out there with no alternative to the public restroom. Thankfully there was no real harm done and looking back, I can find the humor in these bathroom encounters.

Bathroom Counseling

WE PULLED into the gas station to fill up and of course I had to go to the ladies' room. We were on our way to Missouri to visit family and it was a dreaded two-day trip that my husband and I do every year. Not that we dreaded seeing family, but neither of us enjoy long days in the car.

I went in while he was going through the ritual of getting the gas. Shortly after entering my stall, I heard someone else enter and I could see her spiked heels under the door. As she went into the adjoining stall, she dropped her purse and was cursing and mumbling to herself. Her lipstick rolled under into my space and I grabbed it and handed it back under the wall. She didn't say anything for a moment and then she asked if I could hear her.

"Uh, yes, I can hear you," I replied.

"Thank God. I really need to talk." She sounded young and desperate. "I'm having the day from hell! The honest to God day from HELL!" She sounded really frustrated.

"Oh, I'm so sorry," I replied. I thought perhaps this young lady might need a little consoling, and with my experience as a trained counselor, who better to lend a listening ear. And besides, I was sort of a captive audience for the moment anyway.

She continued, "I thought I was going to pee in my pants before I got in here. My head is killing me and I just want to scream."

"Try taking a few deep breaths and just relax. That always..."

She interrupted me in mid-sentence. "Really! Let me tell you what happened."

I was right, this girl needed a little motherly love. "OK, if you think that will help," I offered.

"I thought I would surprise Jeff this morning with an early morning visit."

Now I had to wonder, who's Jeff?

She continued, "It was a surprise all right! I have a key and unlocked the door thinking I would just slip into his bed. Well get this!" she said. "There wasn't room, because some hussy was already in his bed!"

I'm thinking to myself, I bet that was a big surprise for

everyone involved. This was beginning to be a story that might need a different kind of consoling than you get from talking to a motherly listening ear.

"Well I screamed, Jeff screamed and that bitch just covered up her head. Big damn surprise...for me! Can you believe it?" Her voice was loud and high pitched.

"Oh my," was all I could manage to say at that point. And with that I flushed my commode and decided this counseling session might need to come to an end for me. She continued to rant as I headed to the sink to wash my hands.

She continued in a calmer voice but talking faster. "I said, 'What the hell is going on here?' And he just kept saying 'Calm down honey, I can explain.' 'What's to explain,' I yelled. 'You have another woman in your bed.'" I totally lost it." She was a little out of breath at that point.

So I said, "That had to be disconcerting, I'm sure."

"I wanted to kill the bitch! Pull her hair out. Punch her in the face."

I guess my comment had been a bit of an understatement. I tried another approach. "I understand, you were really angry and understandably so. I hope your day gets better but I should probably..."

She interrupted again. "No, listen to this! I was so totally pissed. I threw the lamp at his head and marched right out of there. I slammed the door so hard it might have broken."

I wasn't sure if she was referring to breaking the door, his head or the lamp. "I hope no one was hurt," I said as I reached for a paper towel to dry my hands. I thought it was time for me to leave. "I was totally hurt. What should I do now?" she asked in a rather pitiful voice.

Now I was caught up again. How could I just walk out when she was asking me for help? "Well, maybe just give yourself a little time to cool off. This is obviously very fresh pain." There is silence from the next stall, so I went on, "And then perhaps you can talk to Jeff and work things out." I thought that was sound advice and a good stopping point and reached for the door handle.

"I don't ever want to see him again." Now she started to cry.

"Oh, don't cry. He's just not worth your tears, honey, if he's going to be unfaithful. Better to find out what a loser he is now before it's too late." So much for my objective listening ear.

"But I think I love him," she sobbed.

"Now that's a problem. Maybe it was better when you were angry at him," I said as much to myself as to her. I knew I should probably leave... and I wanted to leave, but my nurturing instincts were working overtime.

She started again through her tears. "I never saw her face. She jerked the sheet over her head. I hope the lamp hit her."

"Well, he's the one who let her into his bed, so bash him," I offered, losing all professional counseling demeanor. I was getting way too caught up in this tale of woe.

"Don't call him a bastard! It was that bitch in his bed that's causing the problem!" she yelled.

Now I was at a loss for words. There was a brief silence and then she said the strangest thing.

"Wait a minute, do you know who was in his bed?"

"Who me? Lord no. I don't know Jeff, or you... so how could I know who was in his bed." This was getting weird.

"You know, don't you? Tell me! I want to know! I need to know." She was sounding hysterical and suddenly I was the target of her anger.

"Calm down honey. You're not making sense. Breathe, just breathe." I was trying to remain calm and soothing.

She actually seemed to get a little control when she said, "Listen, you need to tell me who was in Jeff's bed. You're my friend, my best friend."

"I've never even met you! I just had to go to the bathroom and you came in here all hysterical. I've been trying to help but I think I should go now. Do you want me to call someone for you?"

"Please don't leave me hanging. If you know just tell me. Can't you feel my pain? I need you to be my friend." Now she was sounding desperate again.

"I'm sorry, but I don't think I can help. I have to go. My husband is waiting out in the car by now. Do you want me to get the lady who works here? She might know who to call," I asked rather feebly.

"Who?" She was yelling now as she flushed her commode. "NO, I'll kill her. I will kill her!"

Had this girl gone completely mad? What in the world had I gotten into? I finally managed to say in a shaky voice, "I think you need professional help. And I'm not it!"

"Hold on a sec," she said. "Hey, could you keep it down over there?"

"What?" I was totally confused. "Me? You want me to be quiet now?"

"Yes you. I can't even think straight with your babbling."

"My babbling? You...you said you needed to talk. I

was just trying to help. You seemed so ...needy." This was too bizarre for words.

"What the hell are you talking about? Look lady, I've had a really bad day and it's not even noon yet. I don't need any more crap on my plate. So just shut up and leave me alone." She actually banged her fist on the wall of her stall!

It was most definitely time for me to leave. We nearly collided as she came out of the stall holding a cell phone to her ear.

"I'm sorry, Michelle, this old lady in the next stall has been talking to herself ever since I came in here and called you. Seriously... just blabbing the whole damn time I've been talking to you. God, you find all kinds of weirdos in a public bathroom."

She looked at me, checked her lipstick in the mirror smeared on some lip gloss and never missed a beat. "So it was Melanie in his bed! I should have known! What a loser! I'm definitely gonna kick her butt and I'm totally done with him. I'm over it! Hey, you wannna hang out tonight?" And with that she opened the door and left the ladies' room.

She had been on her cell phone with her friend Michelle the entire time I thought she was talking to me. And I was the weirdo in the ladies' room! Perhaps I needed counseling.

Several years later, I was on a shorter road trip by myself. Unfortunately, it wasn't short enough to avoid an urgent need at a rest stop.

Bathroom Misunderstanding

I DON'T NORMALLY TAKE LONG DRIVING trips by myself, but I was going to meet a friend for a three-day reunion in the North Carolina mountains. I armed myself with snacks and a small cooler filled with soft drinks and some CDs with my favorite '60s music. I was snacking and drinking and singing my way down the highway when the urge hit me. I needed a bathroom and I needed it sooner rather than later. So much for packing that many drinks.

The sign read Rest Stop 2 Miles. I looked at my speedometer and nudged my speed a bit to get there faster. I pulled into the parking lot, got out, locked the car, and headed for the ladies' room. It had a sign that read Out of Order. How could they advertise a rest stop where the ladies' room is out of order?

I don't know if men have this issue, but when my mind says I can go potty soon, my body totally expects to get it done…soon. The minute I pull into my driveway at home, it is a given, the first stop in the house will be the bathroom. And now the ladies' room was not available! I was desperate.

I ran around to the men's room. I knocked just to be sure, but I heard nothing, so I went in. There was the urinal, but of course I dashed for the stall with the door. With great relief I began the ritual of taking down my pants, trying desperately to keep my pant legs from hitting the floor while I balanced above the commode. At least men can stand straight up at a urinal. I always hear Mom's voice from my childhood warning NOT to sit on a public toilet seat. Has anyone ever actually gotten a vene-real disease from a toilet seat?

As I juggled my purse and my pants and reached for the toilet paper roll I heard the door open to the men's room. Now I wasn't alone. I saw his shoes and hoped he didn't look at mine.

"Beautiful day out there," he said. "I been on the road for a long time. How about you?"

Was I going to have to answer him? Maybe he'll leave soon. Maybe he was on his cell phone like my previous encounter on the trip to Missouri. Finally, I pitched my voice a little lower and said, "Yup."

"I been in that pick up five hours and have five more to go. You know of any good places to eat close to the highway?"

Oh great, a talker. "Nope," I said again with my lowered voice. I really wanted to get out of any further conversation, remembering how the past conversation had gone when I was talking from a bathroom stall.

Maybe I could just slide around his back and dash out the door. I was feeling totally embarrassed at this point. I struggled to get my pants pulled up while still holding my purse. I used my foot to hit the flush bar. I needed to get out of there. I tried to peak out of the stall. I made my move just as he turned around with his hand on his zipper. I froze. Why didn't I just keep going? But I just froze, and he started looking me up and down.

Oh my God, I'm stuck in the men's room with a sexual predator! Frightening pictures of what might happen next flashed through my head like a horror movie. But I still couldn't move.

"Hot dang, I forgot I'm in North Carolina," he said as

he continued checking me out from head to toe. "You're the first one of...you know...uh, your kind I've seen."

"What?" I managed to stammer. What did being in North Carolina have to do with anything? Didn't they have women where he came from?

"And you look really good. I mean uh... for a...uh..." Now he was at a loss for words. He really didn't appear to be very threatening.

I no longer felt threatened, but I was still standing frozen against the wall when I said, "I'm so sorry. I just really had to go, and I forgot to lock the door."

"Oh no, it's perfectly ok. I'm a law-abiding man, and see you are too. I understand you didn't have a choice but to come in here. No harm. 'specially since we were both born with the same equipment." He was now the one who seemed embarrassed and trying to make light of an awkward situation, but I was a little confused.

"No, I just HAD to come in here and use this bathroom because I couldn't use the other one." And then it occurred to me what he was thinking. "Oh God," I gasped.

"No, it's OK, really. I totally understand it's the law." He reached out and gave my shoulder a little punch like guys do. "Oh sorry. Maybe ya'll don't do that." He folded his arms across his body not knowing what to do next. Well, I didn't know what to do either. I honestly didn't know whether to laugh or cry. I was just glad he wasn't the bad guy I guessed him to be earlier.

"I hope you don't mind me asking, but I'm just naturally the curious type. Have you had any surgeries yet, cause you look like a real woman...uh and well... those look dang good too." He was staring straight at my chest.

"NO... I mean Yes, these are mine. I AM a real woman," I tried to explain.

"Of course you're a woman...if you want to be. I didn't mean to offend you. You just have to understand I'm not familiar with your kind. I'm tryin' to keep an open mind. Live and let live...that's what I say."

"Well yes, I agree, but I'm not that kind...not one of... NOT whatever you might be thinking.

He interrupted me. "I get it. The law says you had to use this bathroom because of your birth certificate. For what it's worth, I honestly don't think you would be a threat in the ladies' room. Who would even know if you were in a stall?"

"Of course I'm not a threat! I had to use THIS bathroom because I couldn't go in the other one and I was desperate." This whole conversation was getting crazy. "Now I really need to go!"

"Again? Lordy, you might have an enlarged prostate. It'll cause you to feel like you have to pee again right after you just did. My Daddy had that issue. Go right ahead and try." He gestured toward the urinal.

"I don't have a prostate!" I shouted at him.

"Well fine, that's why I asked you if you already had the surgery. Now I guess they gave you a tiny bladder just like a woman." He was laughing now.

"Seriously, I have to go...leave. And I'm not...I don't have a...oh never mind," I said.

"Yes sir...uh, ma'am. See, I'm catching on to this thing. Wait till I tell the folks at home I shared a bathroom with one of your kind in North Carolina. They will never believe it. Guess this was just my lucky day after all. Can I take a picture with you?" he asked seriously.

"NO!" I responded harshly as I rushed past him.

"Have a nice day, and tell your surgeon he did a fantastic job. Shucks, I'd a never guessed if you hadn't been in the men's room," he said as I left. And then I heard him say to himself, "Dang, he looked just like a woman to me."

I swear, I will never go into another men's room as long as I live...at least not in North Carolina.

Actually, I would avoid public restrooms altogether if I could, but I can't so I guess I'll just have to go with the flow. Now that is bathroom humor!

∾

CHARLOTTE HACKMAN IS AN AUTHOR, playwright, and actress who has lived in Wilmington since 1993. Her first nonfiction book, The Strength To Let Go, was published in 2015 under the pen name Jo Henry. Her play Change of Life was produced off-Broadway in New York. After moving to Wilmington, Charlotte served as President of the board of Big Dawg productions for several years. Her acting resume includes credits from major movies, TV series, and the stage. Charlotte enjoys playing poker, writing, painting, and traveling. Much of her writing takes place during summers in the North Carolina mountains.

THE SARPY COUNTY INCIDENT

KENNETH VEST

J ake Travis was going to have a lousy week. He was a general assignment and live reporter for the number one TV station in Omaha. WTOT-TV had a great reputation and was keenly watched by executives at CBS News. The network often counted on the station to back up its Chicago bureau covering the midwest, and reporters who worked there knew they were being watched.

He loved working at Channel 5. It was a lively and ambitious news room and boasted six of the most brilliant news photographers in America. And then there was Big Al Taylor, the worst shooter in the history of television news. He was also very chatty. In fact, he could talk the horns off a goat and was only rarely on the topic at hand. It was Jake's hard luck to draw Big Al as his shooter for most of the upcoming week.

He awakened thinking about the day's piece and how dreary it was going to be. The Douglas County Commissioners were meeting on new zoning and plumbing regulations. What was the news in that? And what video misery was Big Al going to create from a simple meeting?

With Al behind the lens he prayed his producers wouldn't force him to put together a full package, with a stand-up close. He was hoping to talk them into an anchor reader with a soundbite. Jake was trying to shake it out of his troubled mind, as he came downstairs and saw his wife Audrey watching Tom Brokow interview Teddy King on the Today show. He was making the rounds of the morning shows to talk about his nomination for an Emmy as Best Actor in a TV Movie. The Emmy Award show was set to air that Sunday night.

"My God, there he is," Jake said.

"Yes indeed," replied his wife Audrey. "You must be proud of him?"

"Yes I am. He deserves it. He's been plugging away for a long time, seven or eight years, "he sighed.

Jake knew that of all his classmates Teddy had the vision and the determination to go to New York and stick with it until he got his break. He was proud. Teddy was an outstanding, actor. That was the main thing, and he had talent and drive. That's what made the difference.

But it didn't make his day any easier to take. Jake had come to terms with giving up on his dream to become an actor. His life was just fine.

"He looks good like he belongs on that set with Brokow. Me, I get to be on a set with Pauline around five o'clock tonight talking about County Commissioners and their vote on new water regulations for toilets.

"We must cut down on the flushing," Audrey joked

"Hey and no jokes about my career, I know where I am."

Later in the newsroom, Jake got the good news that he didn't have to produce a full package on toilets; the six o'clock producer wanted a brief voiceover. But Jake would still have to cover the meeting and then put together a piece given to him by the assignment editor.

Unlike his friend and fellow TV reporter Joe Dixon, Jake Travis treated his assignment editor, Allison Pearsall, with an enormous amount of respect. She had immense power over Jake and the other reporters in the newsroom. Her daily decisions determined what the reporters covered, how important they were to the newscast, and thus how high in the order of the rundown. While reporters would often groan when given the latest topic on the economy, they silently dreaded yet another snoozer that would never make it on their an audition reel, their main hope to jump to a larger market.

So Jake was always courteous no matter how disappointed he was. He was even solicitous and quite charming to Allison. Jake had already received more than his fair share of sidebars on the dismal state of the American economy, from short-term interest rates to small appliance sales and the area housing market. He accepted them all graciously and did his best to make the packages interesting, even though they were far from compelling. At the same time Jake was always pitching alternative stories he argued were more interesting and of greater significance to viewers. He rarely won, but always remained friendly and collegial no matter how pissed he was.

On the other hand, Joe was rude and arrogant, often refusing her proposed stories. This morning she had given him a piece on the opening of the new water treatment plant. He took the assignment sheet she handed him, waded it up into a ball and dropped it on her desk. After a brief but tense discussion, Allison made a bargain with Joe. If he produced the water treatment story, the following day he could work on his three-part series on the impact of farm chemicals on the region's water supply.

Jake was flabbergasted. Joe was rewarded for being arrogant and rude. Why didn't being nice and supportive give him an advantage?

Plus, WTOT-TV was in Omaha, Nebraska, surrounded by corn farmers who relied on the chemicals Joe was about to denounce. Those chemical companies also spent a lot of money advertising on their station at this time of the year. Joe didn't care. In fact, he enjoyed pissing them off.

And it was especially galling to Jake that his assignment that day was to cover the 15th anniversary of the death of Elvis Presley. Big Al would be his photographer. He was to interview Carla Mae Shelton about her sorrow for the departed "King." He had to produce a wrap for the six o'clock and an on-camera talk back with the anchor on the five at live show.

As they drove to Carla Mae's house big Al was giving Jake the lowdown on how to retire early from the TV news business and get rich on coupons. After ten minutes of learning about the real deal on how to make money from retail and grocery stores, Jake interrupted to talk about the assignment.

"Say, Al, let's make sure we're in sync on this one. Let's get some video of her paying homage to Elvis in her shrine. Then be sure to get some shots of all the stuff she's bound to have hanging on the wall, OK?"

"You can count on me chief. Hand-held or sticks?"

Big Al was well known for shooting some of the shakiest video in the profession. Reporters assigned to work with him joked that he often used the "Titani-cam" because the picture would often dip below the horizon; and he was also noted for "trombone-zooms" pushing the focal point in and out quickly as if he were playing a jazz instrument.

"Uh, let's go with a tripod for all of this. And we'll shoot a stand-up close outside the house. Yo! Here we are."

The instant Jake saw Carla Mae Shelton greeting

them at the door he knew this was going to be a great feature story after all. She was 56 years old and looked as if she had lived each one of those years as hard as possible. Her dirty blonde hair was piled on her head like a bird's nest designed by a mad scientist, a long cigarette dangled from her ruby lips and she wore with pride an Elvis T-shirt.

"Y'all come in. Do you want a tour of the house?" Just as Big Al was about to say God knows what, Jake spoke up declining the tour and asking to head to the shrine. He explained they were on a tight deadline, smiling as he told her she was going to star on the Six O'clock news.

"Oh My. Well, I hope I look OK. If I'm to represent the Elvis fans of Omaha I want to make sure I'm presentable. It's quite an honor. So many of us still love the 'King',"

"You look wonderful Carla Mae. I can't wait to see you on TV," Jake said with a smile.

And then he saw the shrine and almost fell to his knees to praise whatever television God had decided to hand him this visual delight. She had turned the better half of a small office to memorabilia of the late superstar. Standing in the corner was a full-size plastic statue of Elvis, captured in the early days when time had stopped for his fans. Surrounding him, behind and on either side there were pictures, posters and postcards. Multi-colored ribbons adorned the walls; Carla Mae had won them in Elvis adoration contests at meetings and conventions all over the country.

There were dozens of pictures of her and Elvis impersonators organized by the quality of each one's performance. There was so much it would have taken hours, and Jake only had 90 seconds to tell this story, there was no need to get too much. So he made sure Big Al shot for only about twenty minutes, getting enough wide shots, and video of some of the pictures, posters and the rest of the memorabilia.

Now it was time for the interview and he arranged the shot with Carla Mae sitting in a chair with the statue looking over her shoulder. Jake began with the easy questions, when was the first time she had seen Elvis, what was it like, how many of her girlfriends still adored the great singer. He got a few more details and then it was time for the money question and the response he was hoping to receive.

"So Carla Mae, with all that Elvis meant to you, for all the years you've have mourned his loss, on this day of his untimely death, how does it make you feel?"

She had been jovial and chatty until now, but the question hit her hard. Her face blanched, and her eyes welled up. She shook her head, as if to say it can't be true, he's not really gone, and then she began to speak as the tears streamed down her face.

"I still can't believe it after all these years. . ."

Suddenly, from behind him, there was the unmistakable hissing sound of the camera shutting down. Jake turned around in horror as Big Al lowered the camera lens and with a look of deep empathy for Carla Mae he tried to comfort her.

"Darlin', ain't no reason to cry. I know he's gone, dead and left this world a long time ago. But he's at peace now with the angels above and our sweet lord. I..."

Jake was standing now with his back to Carla Mae he whispered violently to Big Al.

"Get that camera rolling again now and don't say

another word or I will have you fired."

Al shrugged his shoulders and fired up the camera and Jake tried to get Carla Mae back to where she was but it was no use. He returned to some neutral questions trying to build her up to the magic moment again but she was through mourning in public and the interview ended when she said, "I won't cry again. I done it once. Not going to again."

Jake was furious as they packed up and headed outside for the stand-up close. He was incensed that Allison had assigned him this story to begin with and then burdened him with Al. As for his jocular camera-man, Jake felt a knife to the heart was the only answer. When they were outside the house looking for a spot to set up for the close, Jake let him have it.

"I can't think of a more unprofessional, idiotic and deranged action in my entire career. You do realize you screwed the pooch on this story beyond any hope of redemption?"

Big Al continued to set up the tripod in silence with a puzzled look on his face. Then it hit him.

"Oh, you was goin' for the emotional thing, you wanted her to cry! Why didn't you say so?"

"Ya think! Holy Christ, Al, you never belong in a story, ever. You never have the right to say anything during an interview?"

"I getcha. Never happen again," he said brightly. "Look we got the first part. I think we can make it work, hey?"

Jake mumbled to himself as he walked to the spot where he would voice the closing stand-up.

"OK, let's make this in one take, please. We need to

get back and see how much of a disaster this is going to be."

"Sure thing, Kid."

"Three-two-one: And so Carla Mae Shelton and hundreds of thousands of fans pause on this day to honor their rock-and-roll hero. To them he is still alive today as he was so many years ago. But as bittersweet as this anniversary is, Elvis fans should take comfort. He might be dead, but he's not gaining weight anymore. Jake Travis, Action News."

Jake threw the microphone to the ground and got into the crew-car to start writing his script. When Big Al got behind the wheel he looked at Jake and shook his head.

"You know that close is going to get you into trouble."

"Shut the hell up and drive," Jake muttered.

∼

AFTER THE ELVIS debacle Jake's luck turned even worse. Here he was on a Sunday night watching the late news. His story was about to hit the air. He was sitting in the newsroom all alone, with a bank of three TV sets on the wall. His station and one other were airing the news. The Emmys were being broadcast on the ABC affiliate.

His on-air package that day had been another award winner, all about how the next morning, bright and early on a Monday, new bus routes would be operating in adjacent Sarpy County. A major transportation development, he had written about it in riveting detail all followed of course by an on-camera close along the route in Sarpy County.

As he watched his own newscast he noticed that the

Emmys were coming to one of the major awards for the night, Best Actor. That's when it dawned on him that the vast majority of viewers in his market were most assuredly watching the Emmys on ABC. Teddy was nominated for Best Actor for his portrayal of Billy Sunday, the famous fire-breathing evangelist in the 1930s who had also played baseball for the Chicago White Stockings.

Teddy was magnificent, capturing the fiery blend of Bible-thumping and athleticism that Sunday would bring to his hell-raising revivals throughout the Midwest. And then it happened.

Jake's story rolled and he heard his voice intoning about remote bus routes that would now be open to workers in downtown Omaha and at Offutt Air Force base, just as Tony Randall opened the envelope to announce the winner for best actor. It was Teddy.

Jake's story was the only reporter package on the air that night and it had to be long, not to impart information, just to fill the time and that also meant a long on-camera close standing alone on a distant highway with a bus stop over his right shoulder and the Midwestern plains spread out behind him to an endless horizon.

Suddenly, moments into his story, Teddy walked up to the stage took his Emmy and stepped up to the podium. He thanked everyone who had ever had a hand in helping him win this marvelous award.

It was a long list and as Teddy reached the end of his acceptance speech, Jake appeared in his stand-up close on one of the other TVs. Then Teddy came to his final thank you as Jake said, "Jake Travis, Action News Tonight somewhere in Sarpy County."

Jake was alone. There was no one with him to marvel at the symmetry of two lives converging for one brief moment from such widely divergent paths. They were united in time, on television in an Omaha newsroom that he alone would see. There they were Teddy King, the young up-and-coming actor, and Jake Travis, the TV reporter in a medium market.

There were TV sets in newsrooms like this across the country. But it was only there, where new buses would run in Sarpy County, that Teddy and Jake stood together side by side on television playing out their respective roles in life.

He laughed out loud, because no one would ever believe him no matter how hard he tried. Even if people did believe him, they could never feel the moment as he did, saying to himself, "it wasn't supposed to turn out like this."

He knew no one would believe him. It didn't matter. No one could feel as he did murmuring to the empty newsroom. "That was a sign. A goddamned sign. I don't know what for. I only know that it was."

∼

KENNETH VEST is a writer and actor. He is retired from a thirty-year career in television news and public relations. Since his retirement, Ken has written a number of plays and screenplays, including Inside Job, *winner of the Best Original Production at the eighth annual Wilmington Star News Awards. He has also written the plays* Make Me an Angel *and* Naked Underneath, *as well as two screenplays:* Finding Pops *and* Easy Money.

EMMA'S MISSION

SHAWN C. SPROATT

Mid-afternoon. The time before Mom's return from work, but after her roommate, Izzy, came home from her day of taking classes at the local university. Izzy was definitely one of the better roommates Mom had had since moving into this apartment, but today she brought my archenemy with her; someone who made it very clear from the moment she entered our home that she did not like cats.

Sandra.

Just thinking her name made the hairs on my back stand at attention. Every time she came over I made sure to keep a close eye on her. Izzy and Sandra were best friends, which in my opinion meant Izzy wasn't as great of a person as Mom thought she was. Allowing someone who stated that they were a "dog person" and reeked of dogs to enter our home was a major character flaw in my opinion. Izzy and Sandra were only a couple years younger than Mom, but put together they had the IQ and maturity level of a 12-year-old.

From the doorway of Izzy's bedroom, I stared at Sandra, sitting on Izzy's bed with the back of her shirt riding up. Part of her white underwear was exposed, along with a couple rolls of fat that almost made her look like she had a butt crack on her lower back. I considered jumping on the bed and pawing at it, but before I could make my move, Sandra's phone started making an ungodly, screeching noise which caused her to jump to her feet.

"It's Brad," she giggled to Izzy. "I'll be right back."

She made her way to the living room and mumbled something about "stupid cats" as she walked by me. Our rivalry was common knowledge around the apartment, and yet Mom still allowed Izzy to bring her over. Sometimes Mom is just too nice for her own good.

Sandra opened the front door, and I knew I had to make a quick decision. In our building all of the apartments lead to the outdoors, with staircases connecting three levels of apartments. All day I'd wanted to go outside and do a quick patrol of the area.

You see, I have certain times of the day when I sit in the front window and watch as people walk by. I do this to make sure they stay away from our apartment, because a few years ago someone broke in.

We were living in another apartment building at the time, and it was just the two of us. Neither one of us were home when it happened, because Mom had taken me to the vet for my yearly invasive checkup. We came home to find the door ajar, and some of Mom's things were gone. I'd learned from experience that my sense of smell is much stronger than Mom's. I knew the perpetrator was our upstairs neighbor because I could smell his scent all over the apartment. His scent, plus the faint scent of his dog, which is why I don't trust dogs or dog parents.

Unfortunately, while I can understand my mom's language, she can't understand mine. So I was unable to tell her who broke in.

None of my food or toys were taken, so I was more concerned about Mom than myself. She was very upset, and spent many nights after that staying up late and flinching at every noise she heard. Seeing her this way saddened me, so I made sure to stay by her side at night. That way she would know she was being protected. Even though I could sense her fear and anxiety, every time she ran her hand across my back and down to my tail I knew my presence brought her comfort. I realized she not only lost tangible items, but her sense of security as well, because we moved shortly afterward.

My mom is pretty tough, but seeing her so shaken up made me decide that I needed to protect her and make sure this never happened again. I rarely leave the apartment, so it is my duty to keep it safe. It is a job that I hold with high honor and take very seriously.

I have memorized the faces and mannerisms of each person or animal that walks by in case they try any funny business. I also know exactly when they are going to walk by each day. Occasionally their routines change, but for the most part they are all creatures of habit. Most of them seem innocent enough, but there is one dog in particular whom I always keep my eye on.

Most of the dogs that who walk by our apartment ignore me. Occasionally one or two will bark at me, but I never take these as a threat. I know they are merely expressing their intimidation at being watched by a superior species.

There is one dog, though, whom I have my eye on.

Up to this point I had yet to learn his name, but every time he walked by my window he put on a big show of wagging his tail, prancing along with his head held high and his tongue dangling from his mouth.

It was clear he was up to no good.

Every morning and evening he and his dad would walk by my window. Their presence was a guarantee, and the main reason why I knew I had to keep a lookout. However, a whole day and a half had passed, and I hadn't seen either one of them. This was enough to cause concern, so when Sandra opened the front door, I knew this would be the perfect opportunity to go look for that shady character and prove once and for all that he was up to no good. I hated leaving the apartment unprotected, but I had to track down this dog and see for myself what he was up to.

I was so stealthy that Sandra didn't even notice I'd slipped by her until I was a good distance away and I was turning the corner of the building.

I heard her call to Izzy, "Izzy, Emma just ran outside!" I knew I would have to deal with the consequences later. That was OK. I was willing to risk a few less treats after dinner if it meant protecting the residents of the apartment complex.

Mom and Izzy lived on the first floor of the building, so I went up the first flight of stairs I came to. I had no idea where this ruffian lived, but since Mom always left my window cracked slightly open, I knew this dog's scent just as well as my mom's.

At the top of the stairs I picked up the faint smell of his disgusting odor. I heard two sets of feet stomping up the metal staircase behind me. Knowing it was Sandra and Izzy chasing after me, I had to work fast. I followed the scent to my right, which led me up another flight of stairs. I could hear their shouts of complaint at having to climb more stairs, which I couldn't help but enjoy. They both could use a little exercise-Mom was always talking about the benefits from outdoor activity-so really I was doing them yet another favor.

Perhaps a statue would be built in my honor once I cracked the case of the scumbag dog?

His scent started to get stronger, signaling that I was getting closer to his hideout. I could only imagine what evil deeds he was planning while his dad innocently scratched his floppy ears.

Or perhaps his dad was in on it, too? Maybe his dad was actually the real mastermind, and the dog was just a pawn used as a distraction. This would make sense, as his dad had those pesky thumbs and therefore easy access to the rest of the world.

Suddenly, I became very concerned for my safety as well as Izzy and Sandra's. I'd been too rash in my quest, and I'd put their lives at risk. Sandra may have been my enemy, and I hers, but I knew neither one of us wished any real ill will towards each other.

Before I could turn back and lead them to safety, a door just a few feet away from where I stood opened. My nose was accosted by the scent of the evil dog and his dad, both of them exiting their lair.

The situation was even worse than I feared. The dog's dad had his head wrapped in some sort of plastic torture device, preventing him from using his peripheral vision. This confirmed my newfound thought that the dad was the mastermind of the situation. My heart began to pound as my body tensed, every one of my hairs standing straight up. I wondered if this was it for me. Could I be about to lose a battle and meet my maker?

I vaguely heard footsteps behind me, and somewhere in the back of my mind I acknowledged that it had to be Izzy and Sandra catching up to me. I couldn't allow myself to turn around and take my eyes off the dog and his dad; it was too risky.

The dog made the first move. He tried to charge towards me; tail and tongue both wagging. I realized now that his jovial personality was a mere cry for help. How could I have been so stupid not to realize this all along?

Unless this, too, was a trick? Were they perhaps working together?

That statue of me better be twice the size of this building.

I felt a strong pair of hands hoist me off the ground. I attempted to wriggle free as Izzy tried to hold me against her chest.

"It's OK, it's OK, it's OK," she said to me.

"No, it's not!" I screeched, but because she's not multilingual she didn't understand me.

I tried to claw at her face, forgetting that my mom had my claws removed when I was just a babe. If only she'd known the trouble we'd all be in one day, then she never would have taken away our strongest defense.

"Whoa, cool it, big guy," the dog's dad said as the dog continued to approach us. He smiled at Izzy and Sandra and said, "Sorry about him; he loves everybody."

"Too bad we can't say the same about her," Sandra said, and I knew she was referring to me.

"She try to break free?"

"She's usually pretty good. I don't know what's gotten into her today," Izzy said, still trying to keep her hold on me. Didn't they understand what sort of dangerous situation we were in?

"Yeah, he was getting to the point where he'd try to make a run for it every time I opened the door," the evil dad said. "That's one of the reasons why I knew it was time to get him fixed. They say once they start roaming, it's time."

"I'm pretty sure she's been spayed, but she's been in a funny mood today. Maybe because of the full moon?"

My mood was not funny, and the moon had nothing to do with it! All of our lives were in danger! We needed to escape and regroup ASAP!

I hissed at Izzy, and she finally got the message.

"Ok, let's get you back inside," Izzy said.

"Hope your little guy heals up soon!" Sandra waved as we made our way back to the stairs. When her back was to him, she rolled her eyes at Izzy and whispered, "Every time I see that guy, he gives me the creeps."

So Sandra knew this man was not to be trusted. I always assumed she was a moron, but being friendly with the enemy was a pretty smart move on her part. Perhaps I didn't give her enough credit?

Once we were back inside our apartment, I jumped out of Izzy's arms and went straight to my window.

"Don't get any ideas," Izzy said, slamming the window shut. "I can't believe you did that!"

"It's my fault. I should have been paying attention," Sandra said.

"It's ok. We got her back, and that's all that matters. We don't have to tell Katie about this."

I agreed that Mom didn't need to know about today's events. No need to get her worked up over nothing.

Izzy went back into her room, but Sandra stopped and actually smiled at me.

"Emma, you gave me quite the scare," she said as she approached me. "Please don't ever do that to me again, Ok?"

I looked out the window to let her know that the only promise I made was to keep the apartment complex safe.

Outside, the dog and his owner walked by. Neither one looked in our direction, but just to be safe I let out a low growl as a warning.

"You tell 'em, girl," Sandra said.

She hesitated before scratching behind my ears. I purred to solidify the alliance we were making. This mission may have been dangerous, but at least it helped Sandra and I get on polite terms to unite against our common enemy.

I watched the dog and his dad walk away and glared at them. We may have won the battle, but I knew the war was far from over.

∾

SHAWN C. SPROATT is the President of the Board of Directors for Big Dawg Productions. Theater and writing are her two favorite passions, so she is thrilled to be a part of this project. In her early 20s, she self-published a young adult fantasy book and has written dozens of unpublished and unfinished novels. Usually, she can be found working the box office at Big Dawg, but she does enjoy performing theater and, occasionally, stand-up comedy. She thanks you very much for supporting local theater and writing.

SMILES IN STORMSVILLE

KIM HENRY

S he could not believe her luck. She could not believe her destiny. She could not believe her hair was as red as the rattlesnake's tongue. No cowgirl in her goddarn right mind wanted red hair. Black. It had to be black as coffee and bouncy and silky with a kinda natural wildness. And here she was with luminous red hair and her heart belonging to the only cowboy in town who'd lost his smile. It had gone a-missin' right after their last soiree down by the creek.

She'd known the times when it had danced across his face like a heel-kicking two-step around the old barn out back. When its kinda crooked way of appearing and disappearing reminded her of the cream on a slice of cherry pie that would splash on to the pastry and then sink right in and disappear before your very eyes. Maybe his smile had just sunk so deep inside of him that he couldn't find it no more? And then again, maybe he was looking for it in all the wrong places. Maybe. Her boot kicked the dust as she remembered him saying to her, "I'm real sorry Velma, I've gotta go do what it is I gotta do." That was right before he rode off and left her standing there with her heart on her sleeve for the vultures to circle over.

Now she was wondering who it was, that was setting out what it was, that he thought he gotta do. And so pretty Velma May was on a quest of her own. She was gonna track down which human bein' was giving out these rules and regulations.

Who had made her cowboy ride off into the boilin' hot, sand-duned, brain-frying desert, doing he thought it was he oughta do in order to find his crooked smile, when she knew where it was all along? And it sure as hell weren't out there over yonder.

And so Velma-May mounted her stallion, which she'd pet-named Steel, and headed down to the local saloon fully armed and with plenty of ammunition. And I don't mean bullets. Her angry mane glinted like flames in the noon day sun. Little Tommy Tailor's ice pop began to melt away even more ferociously as our fiery lass passed him by with her sizzling locks crackling behind her. "Darn it," thought Velma-May to her hair, "why'd ya have to go and be so extra bright today?"

Meanwhile out over yonder, the blond cowboy was searching the Rockies for his long-lost smile. It had deserted his manly chin down by the creek on the eve of the half moon when the fieriest lass in town had uttered three of the most terrifying words that he had ever heard. And they weren't "you're history, cowboy." He thought he could handle it. After all he was a cowboy and he did have the sweetest voice and the widest hat this side of Texas. But no sirree. It was official. He could not. His shoulders may be broad but they could not take the weight of those itty bitty words.

On the other hand Velma-May's shoulders were real petite but nevertheless, she took one deep down breath and swung open the doors of that saloon in Stormsville, the way she'd practiced in front of the mirror as a little girl, the way the cowboys did, and strutted on in. All heads with their thin-moustached, Stetson-hatted, dusty-booted, gun-holstered, spike-heeled, brown-teethed, beady-eyed features, turned to stare at the lass whose hair looked almost good enough to eat.

"Which one of you cowboys is setting out the rules

and regulations around here?" she asked in her best drawl. Now this kinda baffled those Hardy Boys. They drew up their shoulders and puffed out their chests and looked around at each other trying not to let their confusion show too clearly.

"I said, which one of you cowboys is setting out the rules and regulations around here?" Her twang echoed around the saloon and ping-ponged between the glasses. Still, it was the silence that came up and shook her hand.

"I said....."

"We know what you said Velma-May, for goddarn sake, don't say it again or that dynamite on your head might just explode."

"You're goddarn right it might, cowboy, if I don't get an answer by midnight tonight. Which ever one of you no-good, rottin-stinkin', horse-riding, tobacco-chewing, spaghetti-eating, whip-cracking boys is responsible, you had better meet me up on the ol' hillside this eve or there's gonna be fireworks."

And with that she stormed out of that ale house leavin' a scarlet blur and a little puff of smoke a-trailing behind her. Velma-May could not believe what she had just done. "I do not believe what I have just done," she said to herself. But she was mighty glad she'd done it anyhow.

Meanwhile, the sun was having a rootin'-tootin' time up above the Wild West, shinin' down with a force of the divine. Our fair-headed cowboy was wrung through with his own perspiration. In his earnest to do what he gotta do, he'd left his buffalo-hide, hipster-hugging water container on the bank of the creek, moments after the cherry crowned cowgirl had uttered those petrifying words.

The wise old saying of his mama echoed in his head: "You may be blond but you ain't dumb and don't let no one tell you no different." But right there and then he wasn't so sure as to the truth of those words. In fact, right there and then he wasn't so sure of anything.

And so on he went, past the cacti and the cattle bones, throat as parched as a buzzard's crutch, until he saw a sweet heavenly sight. A heard of buffs were grazing not more than three miles off which meant that there had to be a source of liquid wonder around here somewhere. Off he trotted, following the only conviction that he could muster - to find some water with which to drown his sweltering thirst.

The midnight hour had come by all too quickly. In fact, Velma-May thought she'd seen the sun do a low-down deal with the darkness to arrive a little earlier that day but these events were entirely beyond her control. She headed on up to the ol' hill to meet what could be her final meetin'. The whole town had heard of her request and the dust was nowhere near settlin'. Her blazin' glory shone out like a danger warnin' from her position above the town of Stormsville and there wasn't a darn thing she could do about that either.

Old Mother May had told her just after noon that day that she was a brazen hussy and that she was real proud of her.

"It's a mighty fine question, child. I've often wondered it myself. My Frank's gone 'cause he set off ta do what a man's gotta do and I never got to ask him who in the hell decided that?" She'd sat there knittin' her wool into what was now gonna carpet the fancy new hotel in town. It had started off as a rug for her very own hearth on the day that Frank had gone ridin' off to meet the horizon to do what he thought he gotta do. It was supposed to be a surprise for him when he returned. 'Cept he never did return and Old Mother May had said that she would knit and knit until the day he rode back into town.

Velma-May jolted out of memory lane to the present moment where she stood on the crest of the hill and blinked as she saw a lone silhouette approachin' her, real cautious-like. It took a few more bats of her beautiful black eyelashes to realize that it was young Jake Franklin, who she knew was the kindest, sweetest, skinniest cowboy of them all.

"I do not believe my eyes," she said.

"Before you go doin' anything you may be thinkin' of doin', please just hear me out." Jake was sweatin' real hard.

"Go ahead Jake. Speak."

"Well I'm the one who's been sent to this here meeting because I'm the most 'responsible' one in this town and you said 'which ever one of you no-good, rottin-stinkin', horse-riding, tobacco-chewing, spaghetti-eating, whip-cracking boys is 'responsible,' you had better meet me...'"

"But Jake I didn't mean the human kindness kinda responsible."

"Well that's what I thought Velma-May. But you see here it's like this. When you left the saloon this noon we all picked each other's brains to see if we could answer your question. And Big John blamed Sheriff Johnson and Sheriff Johnson blamed Governor Blackstone and Governor Blackstone blamed Reverend Oswald and

Reverend Oswald blamed Sly Old Brown the alemaker and Sly Old Brown the ale maker blamed Good Mr. Pecker the schoolmaster and Good Mr. Pecker the schoolmaster blamed Old Mother May, Ma to all the children.

So we all went to see Old Mother May and stood on her rickety porch and tried to tell her that we had come to the conclusion that she was responsible for makin' a man do what a man's gotta do. But, and picture the scene now Velma-May, not one of those cowboys could speak such words out loud 'cause even in their stony hearts they knew they was a lyin'. It was all real confusing for us. Then, and you're never gonna believe this, then Old Mother May finishes the row of knittin' that she's working on and she stands up and says 'Gentlemen, that is the last stitch that I am ever gonna knit. The carpet is complete and finished and I think we all know the answer to this mighty fine question, which that glorious brazen hussy has asked. We are all responsible for creatin' this myth in our own times and therefore we can all destroy it too. Gentlemen, be free of your shackles. If you wanna lay down your arms, go ahead, lay them down. If you wanna crack open your sorry hearts, go ahead and crack 'em. If you wanna cry, cry. And if any of you want to learn to knit, knit. I've got plenty of wool 'cause I won't be doin' it no more."

Our cowgirl shook her bloody curls in genuine disbelief and in genuine joy. "Good Lord up above, she's goddarn, wisely, cream-clottingly, stampedingly right."

"I know," beamed Jake, real excited like. "I got me my first lesson on Monday."

And with that, bang on cue in this great wild western

play of life, came the ice-cream colored cowboy riding up the hill like his destiny damn near depended on it.

He dismounted his trusty mare and walked on over. "Velma-May," he was panting like a coyote after the chase, "I've found it! I found my lost smile. I found it in the last place I ever thought of lookin' for it. I found it when I bent over that pool of crystal clear water to get myself a drink so that I would not die a death out there doing what it was I thought I gotta do. And then I had me a thought. A big, bright sunrise-red thought. And there it was. As clear as day and as crooked as cream on a slice of cherry pie, smilin' right back up at me from the reflection in those cool depths. And the thought that I had had was,

I love you too."

~

KIM HENRY is Co-founder and Director of Theatre for All, Wilmington's first ongoing creative arts group for folks with disabilities. She's been making up stories since she was a child and hasn't stopped yet. She says, "If the pandemic gave us any gifts, the explosion of creativity was one of them. Here's to happy endings."

COPPY

GWENYFAR

The worst Christmas of my life was the year we moved into our new house on Market St. It was also the year I learned to believe in miracles.

My parents had just moved us into the dilapidated mansion that would consume our lives for the next 16 or so years. We were living in the only room that had had the plaster repaired, the walls painted, the wiring updated and the floors finished on the second floor – it would eventually become my bedroom. Amid the scaffolding and boxes and drop cloths my mother – who was way past her wit's end with the magnitude of the move, the house and now caring for my grandparents who had just been moved into our old house six blocks away - decided that the one thing she really wanted in order to enjoy her new house was a Christmas tree worthy of the space. She had a living room with 14-foot ceilings somewhere in all this mess and she wanted the grandest Christmas tree she could have to fill that space. No one got into Christmas like my mother. In the years to come she would drape the banister in garlands of greenery, hang terracotta angels and red ribbons from the sconces and make eight-course Christmas dinners beyond description.

Did I mention she was Jewish?

So Mommy got her Christmas tree, enough space was cleared in the debris to put out her poinsettia tree skirt and somehow at least one box of ornaments was located. I have to admit that she was right. In all that chaos we did need something normal, something special to focus on instead of the daily arguments about not being able to find anything and then discovering that your best clothing was covered in plaster dust and ruined beyond repair.

But no matter how stressed out we were with tradesmen wandering in and out all the time and the painter who had practically moved in with us for most of the fall and winter, my dog, Coppy, the sweetest beagle who had ever lived, was probably the happiest dog on the planet. Because the new house came with a 6-foot chain link fence around the yard and after four years on the end of 100 foot chain, he was free to wander the yard and run the perimeter all day and all night!

Coppy had been my third-birthday present. I did not know it at the time, but apparently my parents fought a lot about this potential gift. My father believed strongly that children should grow up with a dog. My mother, who did not grow up with a dog, was adamant that if they got me a puppy, the puppy would die and then they were going to have to explain death to a three-year-old. Obviously that was not something she wanted to do.

In one of the rare instances that I know of, my father actually won an argument. So on my third birthday I had a strawberry shortcake birthday cake with Shannon Ingram from down the street and a very sweet, tiny beagle puppy appeared to be my friend.

Daddy's favorite movie in the world is Disney's The Fox and The Hound. He wanted to name the puppy Copper for the beagle in the cartoon. I insisted, in my already very strong-willed three-year-old way, that he would be called Coppy, not Copper. Because Coppy was an original name.

So Coppy was enjoying his newfound freedom and

was probably happier about all changes in our living situation than anyone else in the family. We became a lot closer during this time. We had always been very good friends, but his freedom and ability to come play with me in the yard anywhere I went meant we had more opportunities to get into mischief together, and my parents were very preoccupied with the house, which meant we were left to our own devices more than ever before.

I decided that year, that I was old enough to buy holiday gifts for people myself. At the top of my list was of course, Coppy. Since we had moved, he needed new dog tags with updated information. I found an ad in the Sunday Parade Magazine for engraved dog tags. You could get all sorts of shapes and sizes. After much deliberation, I settled on a dog-bone shaped tag and began saving my allowance toward the $6.50 the engraving would cost plus $3.50 shipping and handling. I had to plan a long way in advance to have time for it to arrive before the holidays. Eventually I had all my money assembled and got Mommy to write a check to the company for my $11.00 I had so carefully saved. I think she was paying for things with quarters and nickels for a couple months after that.

It arrived with four days to spare for the holiday! I was so excited you would have thought the gift was for me. Next came the even better part: wrapping it! Oh my god! That kept me busy for a good couple of hours as I searched for the perfect box, which turned out to be an empty matchbox from the matches from Elijah's Restaurant! I settled on a royal blue wrapping paper and a big, bright, red bow that was as big as the box. It was so beautiful and I felt so grown up to have done all this myself! It was lightweight enough that I could actually rest it on one of the branches of the Christmas tree like a decoration – which just added to my little girl's delight at the whole situation.

My father has always done his Christmas shopping on Christmas Eve. Where other people plan for weeks if not months and start the day after Thanksgiving, my father very calmly sallies forth on the 24th of December and in the matter of two hours does it all.

This particular year my normally very quiet, soft-spoken Daddy came bursting through the back door in the mid afternoon of Christmas eve bellowing for my mother and dropping bags on the floor. "DIANA! DIANA! The dog's out! The door was open! Diana!" Mother came pounding down the stairs at a dead run.

"Kitty, go get his leash out of the drawer!" she directed as she hurried past me and out the backdoor.

Among the many points of irritation in the far from perfect circumstances of the new house was the problem of the garage door: there wasn't one. The garage is a lovely red brick structure completely removed from the house. It is the perfect environment in which to grow shitake mushrooms: damp and dark with a concrete floor. At that time, it did not have a "car door" part of the garage. That was just open and exposed to the street. It would be about twelve years before my parents decided to allocate funds to that particular home improvement project. For the time being they were preoccupied with the ceiling that had just collapsed on part of the first floor. There was a shoddy particle board door between the yard and the garage that was barely hanging on by a thread and didn't stay closed well. Eventually we would work out a system with screen door hooks to keep the garage door closed and people would have to adjust their schedules to avoid getting stuck on the wrong side of the door.

The door wasn't latched, or someone had unlatched it – and Coppy was out.

If you have never spent time with a beagle let me tell you a little about them. They are happiest with their nose on the ground moving sort of like a vacuum cleaner in constant contact with a trail they are scenting. Once they have a scent they begin this howling-talking that is very hard on the human ear but it lets the other dogs in the pack and the hunter know that they have a scent they are following. Once they have a scent it is like a switch has been thrown in their brain and NOTHING ELSE MATTERS.

NOTHING.

They will follow that scent to the end of the earth. Once they get there they will have no idea where they are or how to get home.

We searched till dark for him, calling till our voices were hoarse.

Once it became too dark to see Mommy sent Daddy back out with a flashlight and a hand full of dog food to try again. She called the police and filled a missing dog report. Of course he didn't have his new dog tags because they were under the tree waiting for him. She called the vets in the phone book to ask if anyone had brought in a dog matching his description. It was Christmas Eve, most vets' offices were closed. She left answering machine messages with his description and the detail that he didn't have his tags.

I cried myself to sleep that night and decided that I would forgo presents for Coppy's safe return the next morning.

I woke up convinced that Santa would have brought me back Coppy and he would be safe under the tree.

I must have been the only child in the world upset to find a stack of presents wrapped with bows waiting for me.

We spent Christmas morning driving around looking for Coppy. We came home for lunch and then went out again looking for him some more. All I could think was poor Coppy alone, cold, without food. And his tags were under the tree waiting for him.

I knew things were really bad on the 26th when Daddy suggested that maybe I might want to write a story about Coppy's big adventure.

No, I shook my head, thinking, You just told me that you think he is dead.

The 27th came and went with more searching and no clues.

This was the 1980s. Computers were just starting to be used for recordkeeping in a widespread way, but the internet and file-sharing between government departments was still years away. The week between Christmas and New Year's, everyone's on a skeleton staff so Mommy's missing dog report didn't get filtered through to everybody until the 28th. Someone out at Atlantic Animal Hospital by Landfall had brought in a beagle,

Animal Control called to let us know. "Damn it," Mommy cursed. "I didn't call that one – it was so far away I figured he wouldn't make it out there."

Mommy warned me in the car on the way out there, "Now, we need to be prepared for the possibility that it's not him. You don't want to get your hopes up too much."

At the vet's office they took us back in the kennel area and opened a cage door. It was a flattened version of Coppy all right, but he wouldn't come to me.

"He's pretty bad off," the lady told us. "He can't walk." I grabbed him in a big hug and sobbed all over him while he licked my face.

So our new house was on Market Street – also known as Hwy. 17 N, which is an incredibly busy road. Apparently Coppy was run over on Market St on Christmas Eve and the person who did it kept going. But the lady behind them saw it happen. She scooped up Coppy and drove around to every vet in town until she found the only one that was open on Christmas Eve. And what is more – she guaranteed payment for his care. With a smashed pelvis, two fractured ribs and emergency surgery that wasn't going to be cheap. But she did it anyway. My parents obviously paid Coppy's bills and the following week when he was able to be moved, he came home with us to one of the most grateful families any dog has ever had.

I never met the lady that scooped Coppy up off Market Street, but she taught me to believe in the inherent goodness of people and that miracles really can happen. That Christmas she saved more than a dog's life.

~

GWENYFAR *FELL in love with the magic of theater in the front row balcony at Thalian Hall on her fifth birthday. She considers herself very fortunate to have spent every weekend of the last twelve years in the audience, watching her favorite performers ply their craft. Thank you all for the privilege.*

DISCOVERY

EDUARD SCHMIDT-ZORNER

I turned into the Rue des Récollets, which was deserted. On the left, the ugly walls of the Villemin Military Academy. The water of the canal at the other end of the street glimmered in the glow of lanterns. An iron pole stretched along the shore, where anglers were sitting during the day. I parked and walked up the street.

The road carries the smell of motor oil, fries, dust and cheap perfume, but also of fine roasts, spices and the smell of baguettes. It is a road with contrasts and opposites.

A few Arabs stood at a corner, who looked at me with a hostile attitude. I accelerated my steps and passed by. The pavement was dotted with cigarette butts.

It was quiet. Even from the nearby Gare de l'Est no sound was sent over. The background music of this road was the melodies from a metropolis. Humming and singing.

Somebody had recommended the restaurant L'Atmosphère to me. "Petite brasserie très sympa," old style, good food, waiters with a smile. A great place to have a coffee on a Sunday morning, while watching the boats going up and down the Canal Saint-Martin.

This place had a distinguished old-world décor with a wooden bar and big windows. Kind people and good service. No Wi-Fi, no TV, delightful atmosphere, in which one can relax and dream.

I had a risotto made of celery and asparagus with parmesan and the menu of the day, which was filet of sole with lemon sauce and a big bottle of Viognier. Raspberry creme brûlée followed as dessert.

A steaming coffee stood in front of me and I looked

out of the window. A day ended, and the sun was setting. A boat passed by; the lights of the boat were shining on the water and created golden circles.

I had just taken a sip of my coffee, when I saw a bent man entering the restaurant. I could not really judge his age. He passed by the tables and begged for money. His clothes were a mixture of different styles, worn however, a blue hooded anorak showing a lot of stains, brown trousers, the lower part hanging in rags around his ankles, bare feet in sandals. He held a knapsack in his hand. The shoulder straps in pieces. The rest could not fulfill its purpose to hold the weight on his shoulders.

He was nearing my table and looked at me. I said: Bonsoir. He seemed surprised and responded with Bonsoir as well. He cast a desiring glance at my coffee cup. I invited him to take a seat. The waiter was about to show him the door. I told the waiter, that he was my guest and asked the man, what he would like to have? "A coffee and a brioche if possible," he said. I asked the waiter to bring a big cup of coffee and two brioches with butter.

"You seem not to be blessed with the achievements of our society, to put it gently? I know that the philosophy or romanticism woven around the clochards, sorry, our politically correct term today is SDF, *sans domicile fixe*, homeless, that this philosophy provides a wrong picture."

His face showed a sad expression: "There is and never was romanticism connected to it. To have no money, to live in a homeless shelter, if you are lucky to get a space, especially in winter, to sleep under the bridges, which has been made nearly impossible in the last few years by the municipality, to live in cardboard boxes, or on top of the outlet shafts of the metro to avail of the warm air or to look for work in the central wholesale market in the early hours of the day, is far removed from romantic feelings, I can assure you. Sorry, I will just go and wash my hands before I have my coffee."

He shuffled in the direction of the toilet, watched by the waiter and guests, who frowned or wrinkled their noses, when he passed by.

When he returned, his face looked fresher and he had combed his hair.

I told him that he reminded me of Jean Gabin, the French actor, who played homeless in the film Archimède le clochard. The title hero tries to spend the cold season in prison. However, this fails, and he finally moves to the South of France to escape the cold Paris winter.

"Again, this gives, I dare to say, intentionally, a wrong romantic picture far removed from the cruel reality."

He nodded sadly: "That is true. The majority are addicted to alcohol and sedatives or live on the streets because of a failed relationship, loss of the job, loss of their home or a disastrous financial situation. A situation, in which all could end one day. There is no guarantee for well-being. I was a successful engineer, married, built a house, but the factory closed, I lost my job, we had no money to keep up our standard of living or to pay the mortgage, we got divorced, I had to leave my house in the middle of the night, after my wife threw me out, the house was in her name, the way downhill started rapidly..."

"Do you need help? I asked. "I have some clothes in the car, which might fit you, I think you have my size."

"Thanks, that would be nice." He looked down on his

trousers. "No harm to get rid of these rags." By the way, my name is Léandre. Léandre Beauchemin."

After a moment of silence, he drank his coffee and swallowed the brioche.

"I am writing poems and short stories", he said. He pulled a booklet out of his knapsack. A kind of chapbook. "I offer them for a few Euros. They are handwritten. I sell four or five per day."

I took the book: "I had the impression, that poetry is dead in France. Good for you."

I opened the book at random and read a poem:

Life is in death
There lies the man determined and
      resolved.
Was a promise on a white sheet.
Then there were colourful dresses and the
      dark ones,
soaked in foreign and own blood.
When the winter set in and the fire
let crystals melt to tears on the window,
a white sheet again covers the promises..

His poem was powerful.

I wondered, was his life a circle or a cul-de-sac? Was there hope or only despair waiting for him?

He was living a life which a person under "normal" circumstances could not imagine. A life outside the "normal" routine of a house or apartment, regular work, recognition, a family, a partner, friends.

Shoes with holes in the soles, socks which had not been washed for months, dirty, smelly underwear, a mixture of second-hand clothes, and a weird fashion. The constant ticking in his head of how to find a roof over his head for the night, where to get a bite to eat, or work, to earn a few coins to buy some food and to avoid begging.

I had an idea: "Do you know other homeless who write?

We could publish an anthology and the proceeds go to charity, the publication will make you known, you and your problems. And a bit of money would also be no harm, wouldn't it?

How can I reach you?"

He gave me the number of the homeless shelter.

"Leave a message and we can meet," he said.

I drove him to the shelter, when we left the restaurant near midnight. On my way to my apartment in the 9th arrondissement, my head was full of the thoughts kindled by the conversation with this unfortunate homeless man.

Next day, on my way to the office I bumped into Marcel, a film maker. We arranged to meet for lunch.

"Any new project?" was my first question.

"Yes, we want to make people aware of the problems and talents of the homeless in Paris."

"Hold on," I said, and told him the story of the encounter with Léandre.

"Just the character I am looking for," he said.

EDUARD SCHMIDT-ZORNER is a translator and writer of poetry, haibun, haiku, and short stories. He writes in four languages: English, French, Spanish, and German, and holds workshops on Japanese and Chinese style poetry and prose. He is a member of four writer groups in Ireland, and has lived in County Kerry for more than 25 years. Though born in Germany, he is a proud Irish citizen. He has published 87 anthologies, literary journals, and broadsheets in the United States, the United Kingdom, Ireland, Japan, Sweden, Italy, Bangladesh, India, France, Mauritius, Nigeria, and Canada.

A QUIET, DECENT PLACE

ANNE RUSSELL

He sat on the steps of Diamond Head Mental Health Clinic, left leg stretched out in front of him. I crossed Makapuu Avenue. "Mr. Dickens?" He cupped his hand around his right ear and leaned forward. "Are you Mr. Dickens?" He nodded in assent. "I'm here to take you to an apartment." I noticed the second button off his shirt and his fly coming unsewn. "The Leahi District sent me. Mrs. Ikeda must have told you."

"All I want is a place with a good reading lamp." He spoke with a lisp and a slight, indistinguishable brogue. "I don't care if it's small or anything else about it. Just quiet, decent, with a good lamp."

"We've found you a small cottage. It really isn't bad."

"Quiet?"

"Conveniently located." I felt annoyed he would expect quiet. Quiet was hard to come by on the leeward side of Oahu, even for those with money to pay for it. "Where are your things? I'll help you carry them to my van."

Mr. Dickens slowly turned toward the shopping bags on the step behind him. "I haven't much. Books, a blanket, a towel. They took everything else." He rubbed his gray stubble of beard.

I lifted one of the bags. "You told Community Action you were robbed?"

"Hoodlums." Mr. Dickens bent to lift the remaining bag, stumbled, caught himself. "Bad hip socket."

"I'll bring the van over for you." I carried the bag to the blue minibus parked across from the clinic, started the engine, and U-turned to the curb. Mr. Dickens limped behind me as I loaded his other shopping bag. I opened the passenger door. "We can pick up some things on the way to your new apartment. Razor. Soap. Needle and thread."

"I don't want charity. When my papers come, I'll be able to find employment. I only want a place to stay until my papers come."

I pulled away from the curb and drove out Makapuu toward Kilauea. "What papers?"

"I told Community Action. I'm a college professor. Taught English in seven countries. Educated abroad. It's all in my papers, the ones they stole when they took my valise. When I have a good lamp to see with, I can write the universities to send my credentials."

I humored him. "Of course." I turned off Kilauea in the direction of Waialae. They had warned me about his fantasies. When they found him lying on Kuhio with his shopping bags beside him, he told them he was Professor Charles Dickens and English literature was his field. He became agitated at their disbelief. The Diamond Head Clinic diagnosed him as disoriented with delusions of grandeur, possibly early Alzheimer's, but not a danger to himself or anyone else. If Community Action would house him, the police would work to identify him. Until they discovered his true name, he was to be called Mr. Dickens. "You wait here for me," I said, parking near the Pay'n'Save in Kaimuki. "I'll be right back." I took the keys from the ignition. When I returned with the necessary items, he was sitting inside the van with the windows rolled up and the doors locked, his head off to one side, eyes closed, mouth open. Alarmed, I beat upon the windshield.

"Too noisy," he said when he unlocked the door on

the driver's side. "Traffic. Hoodlums in big cars. Had to close myself in."

"I was only gone a minute." I tossed the plastic bag with the toiletries into his lap with slightly more force than necessary.

Mr. Dickens pulled something out of his ear with his thumb and forefinger. He held up a pink rubber object. "Earplug. Use them all the time." He dropped the earplug into his shirt pocket. "What were you saying?"

"Wasn't important." I eased into traffic and drove toward Waikiki. I wanted to help Mr. Dickens, but he was making it difficult for me to like him. He had a certain arrogance not in keeping with his reduced circumstances. Beggars can't be choosers, I wished to say, but instead I made light conversation. "I'm a graduate student at the university."

For the first time, Mr. Dickens smiled through missing front teeth. "Why didn't you say so? I love students. If I just had students to teach and a quiet place to live, I would be perfectly satisfied."

I decided to play along with his delusion. "And what would you teach us?"

"Yeats. Joyce. D. H. Lawrence. Lawrence is my specialty."

"That's very interesting."

He spoke more loudly. "I am done for. As a man you see me in ruin. Some nights I sleep. Some nights I never close my eyes. I force myself to keep sane." I stared at him. "D. H. Lawrence," he said. "*The Fight for Barbara*. He was much underrated for his plays."

"I never studied him. I'm in public health."

"Why, Nurse Broadbanks! Good literature is food for your soul, which is good for your health."

"I'm not a nurse. I'm studying administration. My name isn't Broadbanks."

"That's from *The Merry Go Round*," Mr. Dickens said. "D. H. Lawrence' play." He chuckled. "I didn't really take you for a nurse. Nurses don't drive vans. They carry bedpans."

My annoyance returned. "Since we're talking names, where did you get Dickens?"

The smile left his face. "That's what they asked me at the clinic. They seemed much concerned about my name. They didn't believe I'm who I am without my papers." He pushed the Pay'n'Save bag toward me. "I don't need these things. All I want is a quiet place near decent people, some students to teach, and to be believed. If you don't believe me, let me out right here. I'll take my books and be on my way." He unlocked the passenger door.

"I believe you! It's just that your name is a bit...unusual."

He looked at me intently through eyes of indistinguishable color. "What's unusual about it?"

"In Hawaii. Not Many Dickenses. But Ikedas! Plenty of those."

"I see." Mr. Dickens stared out the passenger window as I drove past the Ala Wai Canal.

"We're almost there," I said. He didn't answer. I turned left into the maze of streets which made up Waikiki.

"You're not putting me here, are you? This is close to where the hoodlums took my things."

I pulled off the street into an alley which led into a

grove containing several small, pink, wood-frame cottages. "You'll be safe here. Community Action leases this housing."

He disembarked reluctantly, stretching out his left leg and balancing himself on his right leg. "I rather hoped to be up near the university, close to an intellectual environment. I don't need Waikiki hanky-panky."

With a key from the district office, I opened the door to Cottage D. I switched on the overhead light. A bare bulb illuminated the dank interior.

"I'm leaving," announced Mr. Dickens. "Please set my bags out on the ground."

I heard traffic from Kalakaua Avenue. Next door a loud argument began. "We can fix this place up just fine," I reassured him. "I'll get some curtains, a rug, shelves for your books. You'll be nice and cozy."

He peered outside. "I don't like the looks of who's living nearby. Couple of drunks. Getting into a fight."

"You don't have to mingle. You can keep to yourself, stay here until they...." I started to say "find out who you are," but caught myself in time. "Until they send your papers. If you keep moving your residence, they won't know where to direct your mail."

"That's true. I need an address."

"You need an address."

He edged further into the cottage. "I'll be here until I get my papers. But if I have any trouble, I'm leaving. I've had enough of hoodlums."

I carried his bags in from the van. Inside one bag I found his blanket and towel. I arranged the blanket across the narrow bed and laid the towel on top of the dresser. "I'll bring you some sheets."

"And a reading lamp." He dug inside one of the bags, pulling forth a book. *D. H. Lawrence.* He slowly caressed the cover. *Women in Love.* He brought forth another book. *Harry T. Moore. The Collected Letters of Lawrence.*

"I'll find you a bookshelf." I put the Pay'n'Save on top of the towel on the dresser, noticing Mr. Dickens' reflection in the dusty, tarnished mirror.

"And a lamp," he reminded me.

"Certainly a lamp."

He moved around the tiny room, lifting the blinds and closing the windows. "I want to keep the noise out."

"You'll be unbearably hot."

"Better hot than assaulted by raucous sound." He closed the last window and lowered all the blinds. "Stay and talk with me a bit. It's been so long since I've conferred with a student."

I sat awkwardly at one end of the bed, again noticing his missing shirt button and the exposed zipper of his fly. "You must mend your clothes," I admonished. "Mustn't give people the idea you're coming undone."

He placed his hand over the unsewn fly. "That happened when they took my things. They pulled at me when they went after my wallet. I can't help the way I look."

"Well, of course you can't." I was sorry I had embarrassed him. It was so difficult to work with clients and not sound patronizing, especially when they weren't of sound mind. I had to walk a fine line, cater to them yet let them keep their dignity. Supplying housing and food and clothing was the easy part of my work in the district. Not being patronizing was the hard part.

"Are you certain you believe I'm who I say I am?"

asked Mr. Dickens. "I want to tell you how I made my way here, how the vicissitudes of fate brought me to this island and thus to your attention."

"It's not necessary to explain." I felt stifled in the tiny, closed-up room. I wished to see Mr. Dickens settled into his quarters so I could return the van to the district office. My seminar at the university was to start at seven, and I needed a bite of supper from the buffet at the East-West Center. I pointed toward the ill-equipped kitchenette in the far corner. "I'll get you some groceries for your refrigerator."

Mr. Dickens arranged himself at the other end of the bed. "Please let me tell you about myself," he insisted. "I must have one person on this godforsaken island who believes I am telling the truth." I forced myself to face him attentively. "I was born in America. Maryland, to be exact. But educated abroad. My father was in the foreign service. I was placed in school in Scotland. Matriculated at Oxford. That's why it is so difficult to get hold of my papers."

"I thought you said your name is Dickens."

"It is."

"But you say you were born in America."

"I was."

Consistency was not an ingredient of delusions. The fact that the real Charles Dickens was born in England didn't seem to concern the Charles Dickens who sat before me.

"I did not think of myself as American. I spent little time in the United States. I took teaching wherever it struck my fancy. English literature is easier to peddle in

foreign countries, strange as that may seem." He looked
at me as if he expected a response.

"I suppose that's because people in other countries
are eager to learn about our culture."

"Quite so." He seemed pleased. "The consequence of
hegemony."

Hegemony. I thought about the word. Did he mean
homogeny? I pretended I understood.

"I never was a permanent member of a faculty," he
was saying. "Tenure, that sort of thing. So I didn't build
up any financial security. No health insurance. No retirement. I thought I would go on forever, teaching here and
there."

"I see."

"When my hip became dislocated, I ignored it as long
as possible. There came a time I was hospitalized, and
after that, the teaching opportunities were fewer and
farther between. I taught awhile in Mexico, then, nothing. With what remained of my money, I purchased an air
ticket to Hawaii, which would allow me to live in the
United States as an American citizen entitled to health
care in a locale of international culture."

He seemed to be thinking logically. "That's true," I
said.

"I had just enough to see me through a few months
until I secured a position at one of the colleges or
preparatory schools. Perhaps Punahou or Chaminade."

I felt myself getting caught up in his story, though I
knew exclusive Punahou prep schools would have no
interest in the likes of the shabby Mr. Dickens. But
perhaps he was telling the truth, preposterous as it

sounded. Perhaps he had been misunderstood at the clinic. "Tell me again what happened to you," I said.

"As I waited on Kalakaua for a bus to a hotel on King Street, I was assaulted. They drove up in a large car, opened the doors, and leapt upon me. They were big men, and they spoke pidgin, and they took everything of monetary value. My wallet. Wristwatch. Left only my books, scattered about on the sidewalk among the dead plumeria blossoms. Then they drove away. A shopkeeper covered me with a blanket and put a towel beneath my head until the police arrived. That is how I obtained a blanket and towel, through the kindness of a stranger."

He was making good sense. Assaults in Waikiki were commonplace, especially by the locals upon newly-arrived haoles.

"It was all so confusing. The police asked me for iden-tification, and, of course, having been relieved of my wallet, I had none. They asked me the names of relatives or friends, of which I also have none."

"No parents? Brothers and sisters?"

"My dear, I am alone. My only brother was killed in Korea. My parents are deceased."

I felt disbelief return. "No relatives at all? Didn't you ever marry? Have children?"

"Who travels light travels best," said Mr. Dickens. "A wife and children
would impede the interesting life I created for myself. I have my students. D. H. Lawrence. All I ever need."

I imagined being completely alone in the world. Hawaii's ohana system was communal, providing an endless supply of extended family. It was too much to accept that this man would have no one who could vouch for him, that he would lose all his identifying documents, and be named Charles Dickens who taught English literature.

"I told the police about the hoodlums. But I had no witnesses. The assailants had vanished. The police thought I was a common vagrant. They whooshed me first to the jail and thence to the clinic." Mr. Dickens picked up one of his books. He caressed it. "All I have now is you and D. H. Lawrence. You see why it is important you be my friend, Nurse Broadbanks. Everyone else thinks I'm a dotty old man."

I walked toward the door, yearning for the sweet scent of plumeria to eradicate the musty odor which now invaded my nostrils. "I'll bring you food and sheets and things."

"And a lamp."

"Yes, a lamp."

"And stamps and envelopes. So I can write away for my papers." He dug in his shirt pocket. "It's gone."

"What's gone?"

"My earplug. That leaves me only one." He pulled a pink plug from his ear. "Where do you suppose I lost it? In your van?" He pushed himself up from the bed.

"If it's not in the van, I'll buy you another pair of plugs." I was eager to get outside into the sunshine.

"I cannot possibly stay in this place without earplugs. The traffic. The carousing. I couldn't bear the noise."

As I went down the front steps, I heard the couple in the next cottage escalate their argument. "I'll buy you another set of plugs." Mr. Dickens closed the door tightly behind me.

En route from Wakiki toward Palolo, I could tell it was

way past five o'clock by the way the light filtered through the eucalyptus trees in Kapiolani Park. The number of evening joggers was increasing. I would have to hustle to make my seminar at the university in Manoa. Taking care of poor clients mustn't devour my entire life. I would ask one of the other community organizers to take Mr. Dickens his food and earplugs and lamp. I had given him enough of myself for one day.

Parking the van at the district office, I supplied Mr. Dickens' address and the list of items he needed. In my own car on H1 freeway, I merged into thick traffic on Dole Street and East-West Road. A parking spot would be hard to come by. I wedged my Volkswagen into a space that wasn't a space and went inside the School of Public Health. A seminar participant was discussing burnout in the health field. This was a subject I had heard many times before, and I knew the only solution was prevention by avoiding emotional involvement with clients. I listened to the litany of burnt-out cases and was glad I had decided to put Mr. Dickens off til morning. His efforts to convince me he was who he said he was had left me exhausted. I would need at least a night's rest before dealing with him further. My stomach was rumbling for supper by the time the seminar was over. As I walked toward my car, someone tapped me on the shoulder.

"Wan' get chili at Zippy's? Dey mek some hot!" David Paho, a researcher in the university's agronomy program, was licking his lips and winking at me. Momentarily, I imagined going to bed with him, losing myself in his surfer's broad shoulders and deeply-tanned chest. After taking care of the infirm and indigent all week, a tumble with David might be the tonic I needed.

"Sure. Fine. Damn straight." I moved into step with him. I took out the VW keys.

"I'll drive," he said.

A thought tugged at me. "Meet you there in ten minutes. I have to run by Sinclair." David held up his fingers in a V.

In Sinclair Library, I realized I had no idea where the arts and humanities stacks were located. My work kept me in the social science and medical sections and left no time to simply read for pleasure. With help from the reference librarian, I located D. H. Lawrence and, bound in green, *The Fight for Barbara*. Flipping through the pages, I found what I was looking for: "I am done for... Some nights I sleep...Some nights I never close my eyes."

"Please do me a favor," I said at the reference desk. "I've a bit of an emergency. Call Zippy's and tell David Paho to keep the chili hot until tomorrow."

The librarian brightened. "David Paho that rips the pipeline?" She began looking up Zippy's in the phone directory, a smile on her face.

Kuhio night life was making its appearance by the time I arrived in Waikiki. The mahus were out, along with the straight hookers. I weaved impatiently among the limousines cruising the streets. When I parked in the grove, I saw Cottage D was dark. Perhaps he's gone to bed early, I told myself, before I noticed the cottage door standing open. I went inside and switched on the overhead light. The blanket, towel, and Pay'n'Save bag were where I had left them. Clean sheets were folded at the foot of the bed. Canned goods were stacked on the shelves of the kitchenette. But Mr. Dickens was gone, along with his two shopping bags. In the middle of the floor lay an empty Primo beer bottle. One window blind was raised, and glass littered the sill beneath the broken pane.

A local boy about ten years old stood in the doorway. "You lookin' somebody? You wan' da old man?"

I bent to pick up the Primo bottle and saw a pink earplug beneath the bed. Mr. Dickens must have dropped it when I was there in the afternoon. Perhaps it fell out of his shirt pocket when he leaned over to take his books from his shopping bag. "Do you know where he is? Is he coming back soon?" I stared at the beer bottle, knowing Mr. Dickens wasn't the sort to drink beer or leave a bottle on the floor.

"Da old man, he pau," said the boy. "No like da fightin', pack his t'ings an' pau. Da bottle break da window, old man no like kine, outta here. Mus' be loco, fall on da groun'. Las' I see, minute 'go, he take off Kalakaua." The boy dragged his leg in imitation of Mr. Dickens.

I pushed past the boy. "That way?" I pointed toward the Ilikai's illuminated rainbow façade.

"'Bout dat." The boy stooped to pick up an object lying near the front steps. "You give him dis t'ing. He drop it when he fall."

The boy held out the same worn book Mr. Dickens had caressed in the afternoon. Opening to the flyleaf, I saw words inscribed. I held the book up to the light from the cottage window. "Property of Karl Diggins." A sick feeling washed over me. I had jumped to conclusions, not listened well.

"You care 'bout da old man go pau?" The boy followed me to my car.

"That old man," I said, "is Professor Karl Diggins. I

am his friend. If you see him pass this way again, you give him a message for me. Tell him Nurse Broadbanks is coming."

～

ANNE RUSSELL HAS SPENT most of her life in North Carolina and it is the focus of much of her writing. She is the author of twelve plays, including The Porch, *and* No More Sorrow To Arise. *She is also the author of the books:* Wilmington: A pictorial history, North Carolina Portraits of Faith: A Pictorial History of Religions, *the novel,* Tropical Depression, *non-fiction work,* The Wayward Girls of Samarcand, *and the poetry collection,* Waystations.

GRENADINE, THE KUDZU QUEEN

WILEY CASH

1942 was my year. I reckon you've heard a lot of people say things like that, but I really mean it. I was the Kudzu Queen. Of course they call me that now, but it's for a different reason. To look back on your life can be a strange thing, and sometimes I find myself wondering if it all happened to somebody else. After all, who would have ever thought that me, Grenadine Purdy, would be the Kudzu Queen of Enoree, South Carolina?

When I was a little girl there were festivals and parades every year on July 4th, but on this particular year things just felt different. People seemed more excited. Maybe it was because summer had come again and we knew that a lot of our boys would be leaving us soon, but they were with us then. Maybe it was the summer heat or maybe it was something else I can't quite put a finger to, but sometimes I think it could've been the plant.

No one had ever seen it or even heard anything about it until he came. It's funny, now you can't drive a mile in the South without seeing it everywhere. It just grows so fast. The writer James Dickey, the man who wrote that movie about the friends getting lost on the river, he wrote a poem called "Kudzu." He wrote, "You must close your windows at night to keep it out of the house." And let me tell you, he's right. Now, I've never met Mr. James Dickey, and I really don't know what he thought about kudzu besides the quote I've got embroidered and framed over my mantle, but I did meet him and I guess that's where this whole story starts.

1942 was oven-hot. The Upstate gets hot every summer, don't get me wrong, but this was something different. You could walk outside and your back would feel like somebody'd hung a wet cloth over it. Plain miserable. I'd just graduated from the high school. I'd been a cheerleader. The Woodruff Wolverines, state football champs. Anyway, the dust bowl problem out west was just beginning to settle down and the rest of the country was finally learning about that evil called erosion. But of course we didn't know we should be scared until he came.

But other people knew. They picked up his radio show out of Atlanta. Yes, he even broadcasted a radio show about kudzu right from his front porch on WSB-AM. He was a prophet if there ever was one. His name was Channing Cope, and he made me the Kudzu Queen.

I said that people still call me the Kudzu Queen, and it's true. Now I make things with the plant: baskets, paper, and things like that. And I can tell you this: They sell. People are always hearing about me and taking our exit off I-26 to see if I've got anything new. I make things with the leaves, too: jelly, syrup, deep-fried kudzu leaves. You can wrinkle your nose, but I bet you'd like it if you tried. My husband Jerry used to think I was insane, but after forty-nine years of marriage I guess he's given up on me ever changing.

He's retired. He used to be a school principal in Spartanburg, South Carolina. That's where we live. But our daughters haven't always taken it as easily as Jerry. They hated riding the school bus and walking down the aisle toward an empty seat while all those little faces were turned and looking out the windows, watching as Dinah and June's mother wrestled down a kudzu vine in the backyard. I'd spread it out in the yard, twist it, weave it, and have a couple of baskets by the time they got home. And that afternoon there'd be those little faces again, watching Dinah and June walk past that same crazy mother and into the house.

It stopped bothering them eventually, but sometimes they still got upset. The worst fit they ever pitched was in high school, when I put the painted sign in front of the house:

"Baskets by Grenadine, the Kudzu Queen."

They called it tacky. I called it business.

Well, Channing Cope came to Enoree and talked to the mayor, Jesse Winkler, and told him about the problems and terrors of erosion. He showed him the kudzu plant and explained how it can stop soil from eroding, and that news just about drove people wild. At Cope's suggestion, they decided right then and there to incorporate a kudzu festival with the Fourth of July. That day the first annual Enoree Fourth of July Kudzu Festival was born.

Everybody knows that a holiday needs a parade. What in the world would Thanksgiving be without Macy's? Lucky for me they city council had the foresight to know that a Kudzu Queen should lead a parade like the one they had in mind, and they decided to hold an audition.

I'd already tried to be Homecoming Queen, but I got beat by Betsy Bloomfield. I don't know how. I always guessed the judging was based on promiscuity because I was a damn sight prettier than her. Everybody told me that. My mother talked me into auditioning for the parade. She said she thought I could win. I think it was really because she knew the Bloomfields were on vacation up in Lake Lure so there was no chance of me getting whooped by Betsy again. For whatever reason, I tried out. Let me tell you about nervous. That was me.

I dressed up in my cheerleading sweater and did a baton routine while singing the Lord's Prayer. I wanted them to know I had good vocal and motor skills just in case they expected me to deliver a speech while waving or something like that. I don't know why I sang the Lord's Prayer. It wasn't like we were church people. We went during the summer because my daddy had his barbershop closed on Sundays, but we never heard anything good. Reverend Summey was too old to save anybody's soul. All we ever heard him talk about was the sin of Daylight's Savings. He would slam his fist down and demand that we get back on God's time. When I was a little girl, I'd always doze off against my daddy's arm during church while wondering what God's watch looked like.

As you can probably guess, I brought the house down. I sang the Lord's Prayer like it was meant to be sung: sexy. I twirled that baton and pushed out my breasts like nobody's business, and everybody watching stood up and clapped when I finished. Channing Cope walked up to me right there and told me he'd found the Kudzu Queen. Some boys in the back working the spotlight started cheering, and I think one of them might've been Natty Pitts.

Back then, I never really wanted anything I didn't have. I never really was passionate about anything. Maybe that's why I always took Natty Pitts with a grain of salt. All through school he was always writing me love letters and trying to walk me home. You know, the kinds of things boys did back then for girls they liked. I never really thought about him being attractive, but I was never the Kudzu Queen before then either.

July Fourth rolled around slow as Christmas. My mother dressed me in a long, white dress and pulled my brown hair tight around my head. She curled my ponytail into little ringlets, and I felt beautiful.

They drove me in the back of a shiny, back convertible Ford. At the end, I climbed up on a little rickety stage and gave a speech about the importance of our country's independence and how we'd stand up to any dictator who came our way. Channing Cope wrote something for me to say about kudzu, but he didn't hear it. He was long gone to some other town, exciting some other mayor and honoring some other Kudzu Queen. He was a guru. A true pioneer if you ask me. When the U.S. stopped advocating kudzu growth in the fifties, I bet he about lost his mind. And in 1972, when the USDA declared it a weed, well, I figured Mr. Cope probably just up and killed himself.

Now, I know what being watched feels like. That night, I was watched. It seemed like every boy in town was there to see the parade, and there I was up on stage in my dress, sweating like you wouldn't believe. And when I stood to give my speech, those little beads of sweat on my chest ran down into my dress and burned me like fire. I knew he was watching. Right after I walked off the stage, he was there, but something was different. Maybe it was the heat, the smell of the fireworks somewhere out in the dark, or maybe it was his eyes and the burning in my dress.

I've been married for forty-nine years, and I've burned for Jerry a million times. That man has given me more pleasure than any one woman could ever deserve. But I've never wanted anything like I wanted Natty Pitts that night.

We ended up walking around the street during the festival, me still in my dress and him in slacks and a blue shirt, rings of sweat around his armpits, his blonde hair shaved close and sharp. We made our way to the park, away from the crowds and the noise, away from the Fourth of July and all the people we knew. We kissed and he leaned into me with a force I never imagined and still can't quite put my finger on. When it was over I went home, my white dress dusty and wrinkled, my lips smiling and wet. They say lovers can't sleep with a heavy heart, but I can tell you that's not true.

That night, I slept like a child's dream and woke the next morning as the Kudzu Queen.

My daughters are grown and married; one lives in Houston and the other in Asheville. I love them dearly and we tried to raise them right. But even now I long for another child, as if something inside tells me that it's not complete, that my story was never finished or a new one never begun. That's how I know.

Natty Pitts came around a lot in the next few weeks, and I knew he was hoping for something that would never happen again. I felt guilty that I had given into him that one night, not that I was a pillar of morality, but I just didn't want to hurt him any more than he had to be hurt. One afternoon, we were sitting out on his parents' front porch. The swing beneath us creaked while we swayed back and forth. Kudzu grew from the side of his house and ran up a tree, disappearing into the leaves. It had already started.

Natty reached for my hand, but I pulled it away and looked at him. I had to tell him I was sorry for what happened, that I knew I could never be with him, not the way he wanted. His eyes kind of welled up, but he fought back the tears, which just about broke my heart. He told me the least I could do was let him watch me walk away. So that's what I did. I got up and walked down the stairs and into the yard, never looking back. I never saw him again, and he never knew.

A few days later he signed up to fight in the war. I never really heard any news of him, just that he died somewhere in Europe during a battle. Even now I imagine him dead on a beach, still eighteen years old, the ocean washing up around him, his face and body perfect and new while the dead scattered around him are bloody and broken.

I didn't get my period that first month. I knew. My friend Jeanette said not to worry because it happened to her all the time. But that didn't make any difference about how I felt. I sat on the steps watching cars go by that summer, kudzu growing all over Enoree while I felt a small child tug at chords in my body, growing, becoming real. The next month was different, though. I didn't get my period but something else happened. I made myself believe that it was a mishap in my cycle, that I skipped a month. But something told me it wasn't true. I bled out the life that had been growing inside me, and its father was dead on a beach somewhere where people didn't even speak English.

But this all happened years ago, in a time I can't hardly remember, to a girl I can't quite picture. And I suppose it all turned out fine. I'm happy. And even now I can look out into the backyard and see the kudzu vines still growing, weaving, trying to complete the circle. But at night, I close my windows.

∼

WILEY CASH IS the New York Times bestselling author of the novel The Last Ballad, This Dark Road to Mercy, and A Land More Kind Than Home. He lives with his wife and daughters in North Carolina.

ACE

PHILIP GERARD

We discovered the airplane the summer after the Polio had swept through town and left Skeeter Fitch with his paralyzed left leg strapped into a steel brace. On that June morning, Moe—who was called that because his mother cut his black hair in a bowl-cut like Moe Howard, one of the Three Stooges—led us down the dirt road behind our neighborhood, thick woods on one side and barbed wire fence on the other.

Moe carried a whacking stick, which was just what it sounds like: a long heavy stick he used to whack against trees, fence posts, and other kids who got in his way.

His sidekick, Skeeter, gimped along behind. Skeeter was pale and already filthy, as usual, from rolling on the ground to get away from Moe's whacking stick. Behind him walked Barry Raines— we called him Brains because he was already taking algebra in some sort of brainiac class at Central High School, even though he was only in eighth grade, like the rest of us.

Except my little brother Robbie the Runt. Robbie the Runt was a puny little puke of a kid, my parents' darling, who always got to tag along even though he was three years younger than me. Robbie wasn't a bad kid—didn't say much, did what he was told, never complained. He was just there—permanently, eternally there. Wherever I went, I would turn around and bump into the kid and he would give me his goofy grin and just stand there, getting in my way. Robbie the Runt was a smart kid, always reading biographies of George Washington and President Eisenhower and the Wright brothers and about how the Constitution was made. But try to show him how to patch

a bicycle tire and he'd look at you like you just landed
from Mars.

At the supper table, our Dad would always get Robbie
to show off what he was reading. Then he would shoot
his cuffs—he always wore his office clothes to the supper
table—and say to me, "And what are you reading,
Marshall?" And he would look at me without blinking
through his horn-rimmed glasses and steeple his clean
fingers and I would feel about two inches tall. I didn't
read books. Books were hard for me. The letters danced
out of reach and the sentences didn't make a lot of sense
unless I went really slow, and then I got bored and started
to look out the window or whatever.

But give me a tool, something with weight that you
could hold in your hand, a mechanical connection, something that bolted on or screwed in or turned a crank, and
I could get lost for hours. I'd rebuilt our lawn mower
twice and even tuned the engine in the Buick when Dad
was out of town on business and he never noticed.

I had built a whole squadron of airplane models that
hung on wires in the bedroom I shared with Robbie the
Runt—not the easy plastic models but wooden models
that came as blueprints and sheets of balsa wood and
linen, and you had to cut the struts and frames and
stretch the linen over the wings and fuselage and dope it
to make it tight, attach little wires to the ailerons so they
moved up and down and to the tail rudder so it cocked
left or right. I bought them at the Western Auto with
money I saved from my paper route. Mr. Rutledge, the
manager, would order them for me special.

At night, lying in bed and listening to my parents
argue downstairs, I'd stare up at the airplanes and watch

them spin slowly in the breeze sifting in from the open window. The streetlights cast their shadows against the far wall, and I'd imagine flying— soaring and diving and looping all over the sky, my fist curled around the joystick, the wind flying past my face, my brother and all his stupid books far below in a miniature world that didn't matter. I'd fall asleep watching their shadows dance across the wall. It was beautiful to see and lifted my heart on bad nights when I lay awake fearing that I would never amount to anything, which was a lot of nights. I miss them even now.

So at the supper table, I would just grin stupidly and say to my Dad, "Well, the new Archie comic book is a real hoot." And get sent to my room—again—where I could work on my Sopwith Camel or Gypsy Moth.

Beyond the barbed wire fence lay old man Saylor's farm.

He never raised anything but a few milk cows and horses, who had the run of the pastures and the creek. The pastures were all overgrown with burrs and black-berry bushes, and wherever an oak tree grew the space around it was an island of high, dense bramble thicket, ideal for a fort. Our fort in the woods had been bulldozed over during the winter to make room for more cheapo houses in a new subdivision. Now all the woods was surveyed and marked off with stakes, and by the end of the summer it would all be gone. So we were roaming farther afield, daring for the first time to venture across the barbed wire into unknown territory.

You could see out across the pasture to the creek, the sun already high enough to make us squint. Beyond the creek lay more pastures, more fences. On the rusty barbed wire hung a sign hand-painted in red letters on gray barn wood:

Trespassers wil be persecuTed To The fool exTend of
The law
by2 mongrel dogs and a 12-gage shoTgun
whaT hain'T loded wiTh sofer cushins

"THAT DON'T MEAN NOTHING," Moe said. "Them dogs been dead for fifty years." Moe was a raw-boned kid with a head that was too big, his mop of black hair always flopping in his face so that he was constantly slicking it back with his left hand. He'd already done a stint in juvy for breaking into houses, and it was a sure bet he was going back someday soon. His father was a drinker and used to disappear for days on end and sometimes come home in a police car, and none of the grownups ever talked about it. Except that Moe was one of the boys we were not allowed to play with.

But old man Saylor had a reputation for being eccentric and mean, and just maybe he had new mongrel dogs. Maybe he replaced the old mongrel dogs every couple of years, like some people replaced their old cars. Once when I was coming back from fishing the creek farther up the dirt road, I had caught a glimpse of one big yellow dog loping along the pasture near the house, and of old Mr. Saylor himself standing on the porch calling his yellow dog home. He was a tall, bony man dressed all in dungarees, with thick white hair and beard, like an Old

Testament prophet. In those days the only men in our neighborhood who wore beards were the hobos who wandered in from the B&O railroad tracks. Old Mr. Saylor looked my way and shaded his eyes with a hand, like he was scouting, and I ran all the way home.

SKEETER UNLACED the leather straps from his leg brace, stripped it off from his dungarees, and stuffed it behind a bush, the way he always did, so he wouldn't get it all muddy—or else his old man would whip him with his army belt—then he slipped between two strands of wire.

Careful to avoid the cow flop, we humped through the brown grass, already greening up, smelling the humid June air already buzzing with flies and sweet with honeysuckle, scratched our way through brambles and crossed the creek on stepping stones into the pasture farthest from old man Saylor's house. Beyond this field there was one last fence and a long drop into an abandoned borrow pit, a big sandy-clay hole in the earth where dump trucks used to haul out gravel and sand when they built our subdivision. But they didn't go there anymore, not in a long time.

The wind suddenly kicked up out of nowhere—sluicing through a kind of natural funnel between two forested hills over the borrow pit and right into our faces. The grass rustled and hissed, and suddenly the whole pasture seemed to be alive and cooler. The wind lifted my black and orange Orioles cap right off my head and I had to chase it down as it cartwheeled through the high grass.

We crawled on hands and knees through a thicket island into the middle of an open space and inside the shady cave made by a rotten pasture oak and all the brambles, and when we stood up and brushed the grass and leaves off our dungarees and tee-shirts, we were staring at a dilapidated barn roofed in rusty tin. There it stood, totally invisible from outside the thicket. We pushed through the double front door and saw it had through-and-through double doors, so you could drive equipment in and out without backing up. The back double doors were closed and locked by a heavy wooden bar.

And smack in the center of the dirt floor stood an old airplane—or what was left of one. A glider without an engine, a big box kite really, the wings faded yellow fabric over wooden frames, the ghost of a bright idea, lying there in a shed overgrown with sumac and nettles.

"Too cool!" said Moe, and we swarmed over the glider. On the lower wing was a cradle for a pilot to lie in while flying it. "Out of the cool blue Western sky comes Sky King!" Moe yelled and sprawled onto it and the struts in the wing crunched under his weight.

Brains said, "Get off—you're too heavy! Jeez, what a fat load." Moe got to his feet. His eyes shone with that look a boy's eyes get when his little brain is hatching a dangerous and stupid idea.

He turned to Skeeter. "You thinking what I'm thinking?"

Skeeter grinned. He was always missing teeth. He began flapping his arms. "Wild blue yonder, man," he said.

The glider was in bad shape, the canvas wings moldy, torn in patches. A couple of struts were warped and some of the braces were cracked. But the shape of the thing was there, a beautifully efficient machine for soaring through the air. I recognized it. I had one just like it hanging from the ceiling of my room: a 1912 Sparrowhawk glider. Two wings, a thin blade of a frame reaching back to a tail section with swallowtail winglets and a curved vertical stabilizer. The little history card that had come with the model kit claimed that the Sparrowhawk had once held the world glider record, soaring for more than an hour off some mountain peak out West. The curved skids on its undercarriage were propped on a kind of wheeled bogey on narrow rusty tracks that disappeared at the back door of the shed—what we now saw was really a hangar.

We had all heard tales of old man Saylor, how he had made his fortune inventing gadgets for the Army, how he used to fly a private plane right off his pasture. How his only son Cal Junior was killed in the Big War and the old man never went off the place again but holed up in the house with his dogs. He built a cabin on the property for his son's pregnant wife, who died in childbirth, and one night he burned down the cabin on purpose. His 20-year-old granddaughter Penny had just got married last year. It was in the paper. They had the wedding right on the farm and none of us knew anybody who was invited.

But I had never heard about any gliders.

The rusty track, like a miniature railroad, ran to the back doors. On an instinct, I removed the wooden bolt from the back doors and flung one of them open. The breeze rushed in and quivered the wings of the glider. From the open door, I could look down the sloping swale of pasture to a small rise, then a dip to the fence, the point where it dropped off into the borrow pit, and a few hundred yards beyond the pit, I could see green grass. I said "Looks like he launched it from right back here, into the wind."

We kicked around in the high grass and discovered the rest of the overgrown steel track that ran down the slope. I walked slowly down the slope and stood at the barbed wire fence, where a double gate had been fixed at the end of the track and was locked by a rusty chain and padlock, looking out across the borrow pit to the other side. The pit had been carved right out of the pasture, and it lay before me like an open wound—sides scraped and scarred, a hundred feet below, the red clay glistening with pools of stagnant oily water, looking like everything that was missing from my life. The wind was steady on my face. That was why he had launched it from here: the wind. You need wind to generate airspeed over the wings and lift the glider.

The rails ran for maybe a hundred feet to the edge of the pit, about as far as I could throw a baseball.

Moe ran to the fence, jumping up and down with glee, Skeeter and Robbie the Runt close behind. "Jesus H. Christ!" he shouted. "This is going to be the best!"

"That crate ain't in no shape to fly," I reminded him. "It's all

rotten."

Moe grabbed me by the collar of my polo shirt. "Don't you want to do something great? I mean something really great? That they'd remember forever and tell stories about? Man, oh man! Jesus H. Christ, Marsh, it doesn't get any cooler than this!'"

I said, "It's all busted up."

Moe stood toe to toe with me, so close I could smell him, sour and rank. "You're scared. That's what it is."

"I ain't scared."

"Look at us, Marsh. Take a good look." He spun slowly around, flapping his arms at the woods, the pasture, the sky. "Where are we going? You think I'm going anywhere?"

"High school," I said.

Moe snorted. "Yeah, Central High. Home of the losers. You, me, and the gimp here."

"Brains will do okay."

"Right. If his old man don't get transferred again." Brains had been to four schools in four years. My parents said his Dad didn't get transferred—he just couldn't hold a job.

"Only one thing an airplane is good for," Skeeter said.

Robbie the Runt tugged at my wrist. I turned and looked into his squinty eyes. He said quietly, "You can fix it." His nose was running snot.

"Wipe your nose, Runt."

He stared at me earnestly, swiped a bare hand across his nose, the little Orioles cap he wore in imitation of mine askew on his crew cut. "You can make it fly."

I shook him off my arm. "You're dreaming, Runt. It ain't a model." But I could already see it in my mind's eye: the restored glider, wings bright yellow, holding the sunlight, as it swept down the slope on a greased track, then swept through the open gate and lifted into the sky. I watched it soar across the ugly chasm of the borrow pit, a quick shadow darkening the glassy clay pools far below, then skidding down gently into the high grass on the other side.

And that settled it. A bunch of restless boys with all

summer on their hands who don't mind stealing lumber and canvas and paint can fix up anything.

What we didn't worry about:

It never occurred to us that the Sparrowhawk didn't belong to us, that we would essentially be stealing it. All of us except Robbie the Runt were already experienced thieves—money from our moms' pocket books, penknives from the Western Auto, Christmas ornaments off lawns.

We didn't worry about old man Saylor catching us and turning us in to the cops. Nobody had been in that barn in years and years, and from the cover of that thicket surrounding the front of the hangar, we could spot anybody coming literally a mile away.

And we never really considered the possibility that the Sparrowhawk glider wouldn't fly but instead pitch into the borrow pit and cartwheel into pieces at the bottom. Not out loud, anyways.

But that's all I thought about.

Skeeter was a great scrounge, and he turned up with two old Boy Scout tents and his mother's sewing box, to fix the damaged wings. My job was supervising the rebuild. Moe and I stole framing lumber from one of the house building sites, a few sticks at a time so it wouldn't be noticed, working at night and dragging the heavy pieces down to the pasture in the dark so we could retrieve them in the morning and haul them the rest of the way with the others helping. Moe stole a can of yellow highway marker paint from his father's truck.

I cut apart the tents and stitched new patches over the frames. It wasn't easy—the fabric was stiff and the needles kept breaking off. My hands were all cut and raw from the stitching. And before we could even do that, we had to shave down two-by-fours using handsaws and planes, shaping the pieces to match the ones we were replacing. Then we rabbetted joints and screwed them together, hoping they would hold. The new wings took three whole gallons of paint thinner, the closest we had to dope. Moe came up with a spool of baling wire so we could re-rig the wing and tail supports.

I took the model from our bedroom out to the hangar and kept it there so I could compare it to the full-sized glider and make sure we were doing it right.

One night Dad came into our room to say good night and noticed the empty wire. "Where's the yellow one?"

"I traded it for a catcher's mitt," I lied, hoping he wouldn't ask to see the mitt.

He said, "I just hope you're not hanging out with that Moe Gargan character. I hear he's been caught stealing again. I don't want you winding up on the police blotter."

I had no idea what the police blotter was, but that was my father's favorite warning. I guessed it was some big book at the police station which listed which boys weren't ever going to amount to anything. You'd go looking for a job ten years from now, and the guy would say, "Can't hire you, son—your name's on the police blotter." Boys whose names were on the police blotter were doomed to sorry, broken lives. Like Moe and Skeeter. And probably me, too. Just a matter of time.

We worked every day, all day, taking time out to wolf down peanut butter sandwiches and Cokes for lunch, then starting right back in.

Robbie the Runt and Skeeter acted as lookouts. Moe cleared the track and greased it with two cans of Crisco he stole from the A&P, then cut the chain off the fence gate using bolt cutters he borrowed from his father's workshop.

Brains did the math: what our takeoff speed had to be, how far the Sparrowhawk would glide on a certain wind velocity, how far it would drop. He set up an anemometer, which he had stolen from the high school physics lab, to measure the wind velocity. Skeeter contributed a windsock made from one of his mother's nylon stockings and Moe hung it on an aluminum clothes pole liberated from somebody's backyard, mounted against one of the fence posts at the edge of the borrow pit.

After a few days of calculating, Brains announced, "I don't know if it will make it across."

"What do you mean, you don't know?" Moe asked him. "What I said, butt-face."

Moe smacked him on the head, the way he was always doing to Skeeter. He didn't to me, because I was almost as big as Moe.

"Cut it out!" Brains said. "Look." He held out a notebook full of equations. Moe and I studied it, like we knew what it said, but for all we knew it could have been a Chinese crossword puzzle. "You don't get it, do you?"

We just stared at him. "You're too heavy."

"Who is?" Moe demanded.

"You are. And you, too, Marshall. And Skeeter. And me, for that matter. The payload has got to be seventy pounds, max. Sixty would be better."

Robbie the Runt, as usual, poked his nose in where it didn't belong. "I'll do it," he said brightly. "I can fly. Marsh can show me how." He was grinning like a moron. "Can't you, Marsh?"

They all looked at me. For once he was right. For once, a runt was exactly what we needed. "Yeah," I said, "Sure, Runt."

~

THERE ARE moments in a boy's life when time stalls and he stands exactly on the verge of who he was and who he is going to be. The light is perfect, a shaft beamed right down from heaven, and even if he is in a crowd, he stands alone. It's as if a chasm has opened up before him, narrow enough to step across, if he chooses to, and if he is sure-footed. But the chasm is also deep enough to swallow him forever if he stumbles. And if he does not step, the chasm grows wider and wider, till he can no longer step across. All that matters will happen from now on the other side of that chasm, and he will lose his chance to be part of it.

It is a moment when he must depend wholly on his instincts, his intuition, that little voice inside that will, with the right word, make him a saint or a criminal. He must step across to the rest of his life.

In such a moment I saw Penny Saylor stepping out of the shadows and into the waning sunlight of the summer pasture. I had stayed behind when the other boys went home. For once Robbie the Runt was nowhere around. He'd had to go to the dentist that afternoon to get braces put on his teeth.

She didn't see me at first. She was wearing cutoff shorts and a white blouse and her head was bowed so that her red hair fell around her face, hiding her eyes. She walked slowly through the high grass straight toward the hangar and stopped when she saw me at the edge of the thicket.

"I thought I saw somebody out here the other day," she said without looking up.

"We don't mean no harm," I said.

"You found the old hangar," she said and kept walking past me through the new entrance we had hacked out of the thicket till she stood inside the hangar. The Sparrowhawk gleamed like a yellow jewel. She laid a hand on one wing, as if feeling for a pulse. "This thing's been out here since before I was even born. My grandfather always meant to try to fly it someday."

"I bet he flew it plenty."

She turned. "No, his boy died. My father. In the war. He stopped coming out here then." She walked to the far door and unlatched it, swung it open. "That awful pit wasn't even here then. It was just sloping pastureland all way across." She swept her hand toward the pit and for a moment I saw what she was seeing.

I wondered whether she would tell the old man, spoil everything. From where we were standing, the rails were plain to see and the nylon windsock fluttered in a fitful breeze.

"Tell you the truth? I think he was glad to have an excuse not to fly it. I think it scared him. I think you'd have to be crazy to try to fly a kite like this."

"I bet it would work," I said, but all at once my heart didn't believe it anymore. All this time, I'd been operating under the assumption that we would only be trying to do what had already been done. But he had never flown across any borrow pit. Never flown at all.

Silence hung in the air like mist. You could touch it and feel it clammy on your skin. Then she looked at me. "You know what I just found out?" she said, looking weirdly distracted and calm.

"What?"

"My husband Bill. He's dead. His car crashed up in Pennsylvania."

I looked her full in the face and saw then that her green eyes were swollen red, that she must have been wandering around the pasture for hours. I had no idea what to say, so I took her hand in mine and kissed it. She hugged my arm to her breast and cried a little, and I was so close, her soft red hair brushed my face. I'd never been this close to any woman except my mother, and it felt so good I trembled.

"It's this farm," she said. "Everything dies here."

The way she said it chilled me to the bone, but I had no idea what to say back.

She turned abruptly and touched the wing of the glider. "I'm glad you painted it," she said. "It looks beautiful. It doesn't look dead anymore." Then she leaned my way and kissed me quickly on the cheek. "Be a good boy," she said, "and walk me back to the creek."

❧

TWO DAYS LATER, on a cloudy Saturday, I watched a procession of cars rumble down the dirt lane to the Saylor farm. The funeral reception. The cars came and went in a pall of July dust and when they were gone I slipped into the pasture and made my way out to the hangar just to make sure everything was still there. Inside the hangar, in the dusty light, I listened to the first rain splatter against the tin roof. It was oddly comforting. I carefully climbed onto the pilot's cradle and closed my eyes, swaying my body left and right to turn the rudder, hearing it swish behind me, tensioning the levers that controlled the wires and moved the ailerons, the way I had coached Robbie. I imagined Penny watching us fly, her red hair unfurled like a banner in the breeze, her face lighting up with wonder at what we were doing.

But I couldn't hold the daydream. The rain drummed hard on the roof now, and my stomach was all knotted with a terrible conviction. Tomorrow afternoon, we were going to launch my little brother over the side of a cliff and watch him smash to pieces. And that would be the end of the world.

~

THE NEXT DAY was brilliant and breezy, with high cumulus clouds scudding in from the west. Robbie the Runt set himself in the cradle as he had practiced, grinning though his silver braces. Moe, Brains, and I took up our positions behind each wing and the tail and gently pushed the glider out of the barn into the light.

"You count us down," Robbie," I said.

"Roger," he said. I heard him take an exaggerated deep breath and start the countdown at ten. "Three, two, one—blastoff!" he squealed.

We shoved hard, walked, then ran, still pushing, Robbie prone across the wing. The glider slid down the greased rails, picking up speed. At the edge of the meadow we let go and staggered to a halt on the lip of the borrow pit and the plane kept going. We had done it, launched the beautiful Sparrowhawk into the sky, right off the rim of the borrow pit,

I watched the ground slip out from underneath Robbie and he was alone in the empty air, frozen, hands gripping the control wires.

Then the glider stalled and dipped toward the faraway bottom of the pit and the bottom dropped out of my heart. I caught a breathless glimpse of what it would be like to be free of childhood—the thrill of it, and the terror. I could not have said it in those words then, but that does not make it untrue. Most things that mattered then were far beyond my ability to put into sentences.

Robbie lost his hold, or maybe let go on purpose, and he tumbled out of the sky to the mud-clay flank of the borrow pit and slid all the way to the bottom before he stopped. The yellow Sparrowhawk spun gracelessly in slow agonizing motion into the muddy pool at the bottom and splintered into junk. Ronnie lay near it, slathered in mud. His high top sneakers had come off. He wasn't moving, and I saw death in his form, and I could not breathe—my whole chest had been sucked empty—then suddenly he twisted and scrabbled to his feet, dancing around in the mud, clapping his hands together and yelling at the sky like a crazy boy. He was all scratched up, filthy as a stray dog, but I never saw him so happy in his life.

∾

MOE WAS RIGHT. It was the greatest thing we ever did. There was no keeping it a secret.

I spent the summer grounded, allowed out of the yard only to deliver my paper route. In a few months, my parents sent me to Catholic high school up in the city, to learn some discipline, they said. What I learned instead —at long last—was the mystery of books, how to spin thoughts into sentences and not feel so alone in this world. That turned out to be the happy accident of my life, the one thing I never expected. Moe and Skeeter went to Central High and we lost track of each other. Brains' Dad got transferred again and he left town forever.

The smashed up Sparrowhawk rotted away at the bottom of the borrow pit, stabbed and broken in the oily water.

The day after the crash, a Wedgewood-blue Ford pickup truck pulled up in front of our house. We were all seated at the supper table, and I could see through the dining room window two figures coming slowly up the front walk. When the door bell rang, I sprang up and ran to open it. Penny Saylor stood there in a bottle green dress, her red hair pulled back in a pony tail, her face radiant with grief. Behind her stood a gaunt, bearded man. Her grandfather, old Mr. Saylor. He pointed to me and said abruptly, "This the one?"

Penny shook her head.

"Ah," he said, pointing a stiff yellow finger at me. "Then you're a little shit."

"Yes, sir," I said, the most honest admission of my life. "That would be me."

He stared at me a moment longer and wrinkled his

nose, as if I were some disgusting creature he had discovered by accident in his barn. "Just don't grow up to be a bigger shit."

Penny pointed behind me to Robbie the Runt, who as always was suddenly jostling at my elbow. My father stood in his suit and tie, a dinner napkin still pinned to his collar. "What's this all about?" He was rattled, caught off guard, and for an instant I wondered if old man Saylor was going to sock him for letting his wild boys destroy his beautiful 1912 Sparrowhawk glider airplane. Mr. Saylor ignored him and reached out a hand to Robbie, drew him outside. "So you're the one," he said softly and bent down closer to him. "You're the ace." He shook his hand theatrically and placed something in it, then he turned without another word and walked back to his truck. Penny glanced back over her shoulder and smiled—at either Robbie or me, I couldn't be sure.

Later that night, when we were tucked into our narrow bunk beds on opposite sides of our room, with the lights out and the streetlight glancing off the ceiling in a little triangle, Dad came into our bedroom without knocking and threw all the airplane models out the window into the trash can. One by one, he snatched them off their wires and sailed them into the dark, and I think he enjoyed doing it. It was awful to watch. I lay on my bunk bed and stared at nothing and didn't say anything but just listened. You could hear each one splintering as it hit the steel rim of the trash can. He said not a word, but I could hear him choking on his anger, breathing in heavy chuffs.

And that splintering sound is the same sound I always hear whenever somebody's dream gets busted.

After he was gone, Robbie called softly, "Marsh?"
"Yeah."

"I can't help it if I like reading books. I don't mean to, you know. Show off."

"It's all right," I told him. "You learn a lot. You know a lot."

"I don't know anything. Don't know as much now as I knew yesterday."

"Don't talk stupid."

It was a hot, humid night, and we lay on our beds uncovered, sweating on the sheets. Those sticky nights always seemed to last forever. Far off, a train rumbled by on the B & O track and let loose a horn blast at the crossing in town.

"Marsh? I've got to tell you something." "It's okay, Robbie. Whatever it is."

"Tonight? It wasn't the first time I ever saw Penny Saylor."

"What?" I was up on my elbow staring across the dim light filtered by the wavy curtains. Overhead, the empty wires swayed silently, released from the weight of the airplanes they had once held. The dancing wires made it seem like the ghosts of the airplanes were still dangling there in the breeze.

"I came looking for you that day. When she was crying. I heard you talking to her."

So I told him my secret. "Old man Saylor never flew that glider.

You were the first." "I know, Marsh." "You don't get it."

"Just cause you think it was a certain way doesn't make it so." What could I say to the kid? I had pushed him down that track, launched him toward a big hole in the ground. If I was really honest with myself, I knew that glider would never get off the ground. I knew what I was doing to him. Some part of me, the part that inspired such black anger in my father, wanted to watch it happen —the joyful calamity of it, the greatness of the awful thing. I was pretty low-down, all right.

Robbie said, "I was pretty sure, you know, if anybody could. I was pretty sure you could make it fly."

"Pretty sure?"

"Well, if it didn't, the joke would be on you. You'd be on the police blotter forever."

That sent us both into fits of laughing. Jeez, what a dumb puke. What a stupid runt of a kid brother. We were all on the police blotter forever, now.

All the laughter ran out of us after awhile, and I was remembering Penny and how I had walked her to the creek that awful day. What I was seeing on her face was more than plain sorrow. It was the loss of hope. The future taken from her. And for just a few minutes, as I held her hand and guided her along the little path and watched her feet stumble because she was crying too hard to see where she was stepping, I was bigger and stronger and better and older than I would be for many years to come, and at least I could hold onto that to balance out the other.

Then I remembered. "What did he give you? Mister Saylor?" I looked across to his bed and he held something up. The streetlight glinted off a little pair of silver wings.

"The real deal," Robbie said, and flipped them across the room,. I caught them and was surprised at the solid weight of them in my hand. I tossed them back to Robbie and heard his hand slap around them.

Robbie was a doer after all. He read books not because he wanted to know about Washington and Teddy Roosevelt, but because he wanted to be Teddy Roosevelt, to charge up San Juan Hill. I was the one who watched and never did anything. What did I ever do? The biggest model I ever built nose-dived into the clay pit.

Wreckage, that was all I had ever made. Me. Just a little shit who was probably going to grow up to be a bigger shit. Old Mr. Saylor's fierce blue eyes held the truth. I kept seeing him, hearing him say it over and over. Then after a little while I was crying. Robbie said, "You okay, Marsh?"

"Shut up," I said.

"He didn't get one of them." "What are you talking about?"

Robbie giggled, whispered, "The Sparrowhawk. The model. It's still out there in the hangar."

The wires overhead fluttered with their phantom wings. "Go to sleep, Ace."

~

PHILIP GERARD IS the author of thirteen books of fiction and nonfiction, including the novel Cape Fear Rising. *He is the recipient of the 2019 North Carolina Award for Literature, the highest civilian honor conferred by the state. He teaches in the Department of Creative Writing at UNC Wilmington.*

ARRIVAL AND DEPARTURE

CLYDE EDGERTON

Adapted from the novel, Where Trouble Sleeps

I n her church office, Mrs. Clark tucked a clean white sheet around the couch cushions. She swallowed several of her capsules with a cup of water, smoothed her hand over the sheet. She had sprained her ankle so bad she needed to spend a few days and nights right there in the office, hobbling around on her four-footed cane.

She felt the very presence of Jesus Christ of Nazareth. The Lord, in His house. The sheets were so clean and white.

In the bathroom, she hooked the latch, sat in a chair, and carefully managed to finally take off all her clothes and drape them on the second chair she'd brought in. The sprain happened Wednesday and it was Friday night. She sang to herself: I come to the garden alone, while the dew is still on the roses. And the voice I hear, falling on my ear, the Son of God discloses. She cleaned herself with a washcloth and soap and water from the sink. She dried off real good with the towel that Claude T. had brought, along with a change of clothes and a few other items from home. Claude T. was her husband.

Back in her office, in her pajamas, she locked the door, and then looked through the window down at the blinker light, blinking yellow, lay down on her back on the clean sheet, feeling all clean. She pulled her sheet and blanket over her.

"Dear Lord," she prayed aloud, "thank you for our

country, and state, and the United States, and our North American continent. We pray for the sick . . ."

~

JACK UMSTEAD HAD PARKED his new '50 Buick in the parking lot out of the way, under a tree. On his third try, he found an outside church door that was open. About one in two churches had one door open somewhere, and very often there was a stocked refrigerator in a church, sometimes a full kitchen, with crackers and canned goods. And he wasn't beyond going through a trash can or two if there'd been a chicken dinner the night before. You could find whole chicken wings completely untouched, sometimes fried and/or barbecued. They'd keep for up to a week. And with his suit, white shirt, and his tie, he knew damned well he could talk his way out of any difficulty--without even thinking.

It was a nice, very average church inside. As he stepped into a kind of small office-library room, he heard a voice behind a closed door: ". . . and we pray for all babies without mothers. We're thankful for our earth, our solar system, the Milky Way, everything in the universe, our beautiful moon, and the universe itself. Help us to love one another and to love Jesus and accept Him as our Lord and Savior. In Jesus' name, amen."

~

SHE HEARD STEPS, quiet steps in the library room out there—approaching her door. Dear Lord, she thought. It wasn't Preacher Crenshaw's walk, or the janitor

Andrew's, or Claude T.'s, and they were the only ones who . . . It was a very soft walk. Could that . . . could that be . . . ? His Own Self? Here in His own house? Did He live here sometimes? Too? Should she . . . should she speak?

"Jesus?"

"Yes."

"Oh, Jesus. Is that You, Jesus?"

"Verily, verily, it is. For, ah, Yes. For God so loved the world He gave His only begotten son that whosoever believeth in in Him should not perish but have everlasting life. All is well. Do not be afraid. I am, ah, come to save the world. And why don't we just talk through the door here for a minute. That would be best."

She heard a chair being pulled up to the door. This could not be. But what if it was? He'd said believe. "Dear Jesus, I have hurt myself. And I'm having to spend a few days in Thy house. I have . . . I have bathed and come to bed." But he would already know all that. She took a deep breath. She didn't want to faint now. This was really happening.

"Okay with me," said the voice—said Jesus. "Good bathing is a good habit. Did you brush your teeth?"

"I brush them every night with baking soda." She sat up on the side of the bed. She had dreamed and dreamed of walking in the garden with Him, alone, but she'd always believed she'd have to die first and go to heaven. Now she was actually talking to him through a closed door. She felt a little faint. She'd never felt this way. Something like faint and giddy and scared, all mixed up. "I just—I just brushed them."

"Then you are making yourself at home, it sounds

like," said the voice. "And what would . . . what would thy name be?"

"I am Dorothea—Mrs. Claude T. Clark. I am Thy servant, oh Lord. Did you hear my prayer, oh Lord?" She stood and walked with her cane to the door, and stood there.

"I sure did. It was a mighty good prayer, too."

Dorothea tried to picture the face behind the voice. She'd never liked hair on a man's face, but she'd never questioned Jesus' right to have it. But all that had gone on so long ago. "Jesus, do you have a beard?"

"No, I don't, Dorothea. I do have a mustache, though. I, ah, shave when I come to America."

"Well, I'm glad, but I also try to understand the customs of the Middle Ages, Lord. And, Jesus, I've always tried to be a good person."

"And you have been, Dorothea. One of the best in this church. Now, Mr. Clark had a few problems . . . before he died . . . no, wait a minute . . . he hasn't died, has he?"

"That's right. He hasn't." That proved it was Jesus. He knew. "And Lord, I knew he had those problems."

"You can call me Jesus."

"Yes . . . thank you, Jesus. He just got too interested in money, too . . . Didn't he?"

"Yes, he did. Money is not something that's very important, Dorothea. As you know. I don't even carry money with me anymore. Love is what is important. Love thy neighbor as thyself. Love thine enemy. But, you know, on earth I do need to get a little money to live on. Love won't by a fruit pie and a Pepsi, if you know what I mean —Jesus needs to eat—and so I usually just stop in a church to pick up a little money. A Baptist church is always a good bet."

Dorothea thought about the preacher's discretionary fund. She looked over at the safe.

"And while I'm at it," said Jesus, "is there a little money in there that you could slide under the door? I have to depend on the kind hearts of, ah, fellow Christians for money. Fellow Baptists. I'm just like everybody else, you know, more or less, when I'm down on earth."

"Well, yes, there's Brother Crewshaw's discretionary fund." Their minds were working right together. "Let me just get it. This is Your money, Lord—your house and everything in it. Let me get up here. You sure I can't open the door, Lord?

"My face . . .my face sometimes blinds people, Dorothy."

"Dorothea."

"Yes, of course. Next time we will work out some protection for your eyes. Yes, I was talking to a Dorothy early this morning. Not nearly as coherent as you."

At the safe, she started the combination on the lock. She looked back at the door. Her hands shook. The safe door opened. She got out the big manila envelope. What if it wasn't Jesus? She would know if she could see him. Because if it wasn't Jesus, it had to be the Devil. She would know the Devil. Her ankle was hurting.

"If you can just slide some bills under the door that would be wonderful," said Jesus.

"I sure will. It'll take me a minute. I'm kind of slow." She arranged all the fives, tens and twenties, and the one fifty, held them in one hand, got over to the door with her cane, bent, scattered the bills along the bottom of the door and started pushing them under the door with one of the cane's feet.

The visible parts of the bills started disappearing under the door.

"Lord, I want you to know that I slapped Claude T.'s hands more'n once before we got married."

"Good for you. He needed it. And how long you reckon you're going to be stuck in there?"

"I don't know." She had a sudden, wonderful idea. "Dear Lord, could you heal my ankle?—if you got time."

"Oh, Mercy. I've done a good bit of that lately, but I'm sort of on the debit end of healing for this month. But if you keep it quiet about me being here, I might can get back in a day or two. You get that ankle elevated in the meantime. I'll be able to speed up the healing some, I'm sure. But if you tell anybody about this, some of God's plans could get messed up. Okay?"

"Yes. Of course."

"Now, I have to run. Peace be with you. You stay off that ankle as much as you can."

"Jesus, I don't mean to talk bad about Claude T. He's a good man at heart. He's been real good to me."

"Claude T. has a good heart."

She had always hoped that. She was so relieved.

⁓

UMSTEAD WALKED to his new Buick. He wished he wasn't alone, that he had a buddy to tell all about what just happened. Some things you couldn't make better. As he pulled out onto the road, he looked over at the parsonage. Now there—in there—was a man with some power. A whole community cooking him chicken and stew beef, and him having to work just on Sundays for half a day, and visit the hospital once in a while. Selling God. But a preacher sure was not free. He was locked in that house and all, with other people—a damn family.

He approached a blinker light—blinking yellow. It was like it was saying a little something to him, but he couldn't figure out exactly what.

THE END.

≈

CLYDE EDGERTON IS the author of ten novels, a book of advice, a memoir, short stories, and essays. He has been a Guggenheim Fellow and five of his novels have been New York Times Notable Books. He is a member of the Fellowship of Southern Writers and is the Thomas S. Kenan III Distinguished Professor of Creative Writing at UNC Wilmington. He lives in Wilmington, NC, with his wife, Kristina, and their children.

AFTERWORD

Thank you for purchasing this book and for supporting local theater.

If you'd like to learn more about these two wonderful theater companies, please visit them online at:

bigdawgproductions.org

panachetheatre.com

Gratefully yours,

The casts, crews, and friends of the stage

Made in the USA
Columbia, SC
13 June 2020